CAMBRIA HEBERT

It's been a decade since a jock fell in love with a #nerd, and even after all this time, their epic love story continues. The Hashtag crew is back with all their antics and good times, giving an inside look at what life is like with each other after ten years of football, kids, and family.

#Fam is a thirty-thousand-word Hashtag series novella, featuring Romeo & Rimmel, Braeden & Ivy, Trent & Drew, and many more familiar faces! Find out exactly what this crew has been up to and where they are now.

#Fam is told in the alternating POV of Romeo and Rimmel and is considered book nine in the reader-loved Hashtag series.

#FAM

A HASHTAG SERIES NOVELLA

CAMBRIA HEBERT

10 Years Later...

1

THE SLIGHT CREAK OF THE BEDROOM DOOR BARELY registered, but the beating of several tails against my legs and feet were more persistent.

A light giggle turned the beating tails into full-on body wiggles and happy breaths from the three dogs tangled in the blankets around us. At the end of the bed, another dog trampled his bed impatiently.

"Domino," a quiet voice whispered, turning into more giggles. "Eww," she squealed. "Slobber!"

I smiled against the pillow, sleep clinging to me like an old friend but not enticing enough to lure me under and away from the little girl padding over the carpet and fending off a million drooly kisses.

"Morning Ralph," she whispered, and the beating against my leg intensified. "Good boy."

I listened to my daughter love on each of the four dogs in the room, opening my eyes just in time to see her pajama-clad body come around to my side of the bed, a stuffed white bunny clutched under her arm.

Her dark hair was tangled around her shoulders, cheeks still pink from sleep and nose shiny, likely from the dog kisses.

Trying not to smile, I squeezed my eyes closed and feigned sleep, going as far as to let out a little snore. London giggled, but I continued to pretend to be unaware of her presence.

The dogs followed their girl, moving around the mattress in her direction and trampling me in the process.

"Umph." My breath whooshed out of me underneath Ralph's well-placed paw.

London giggled, and my lips twitched. "Mom," she whispered.

I snored.

More giggles made my heart light. I would never get tired of hearing that sound.

"Mooommm," she called. Her breath stirred my hair, and I knew without having to look that she'd propped her chin on the edge of the mattress to stare at me intently.

The call of the Anderson blue eyes was too tempting, especially when they filled a face that looked like a small version of what I saw in the mirror every day.

A physical representation of Romeo and me as one.

Smiling, I blinked as my eyes focused on her heart-shaped face whose chin was indeed resting on the back of her hand that was poised on the edge of the bed.

"I knew you were faking," she said.

"I would never!" I protested.

Her wide blue eyes rolled before focusing intently on me once more. She had the same stare as Romeo. All three of my kids did. The one that made you feel like you were the only person in the entire world when they looked at you.

"Domino slobbered on Betty." London informed me, holding up an oversized white ear on her bunny. I squinted at the pink fur lining the center. It was definitely wet.

"And on you by the looks of your nose."

Her eyes crossed, trying to see her own nose, and it made me laugh. "That was Ralph."

Hearing his name, he plopped himself across my middle, thumping another grunt out of me as he pinned me to the bed.

Without any hesitation, he slurped his big tongue up the side of London's cheek. She squealed, and I laughed. "He got you again."

Hearing my amusement, Ralph lunged at me, swiping his tongue across my face too.

London laughed. "You too, Mom!"

"I'm going to have to cancel pancake Sunday," I declared. "I can't possibly cook when I'm covered in drool."

"It wipes off!" London swiped her damp face across the sheet.

I gasped. "Did you just wipe that all over my bed?"

"It goes with the dog hair." She reasoned.

A low growl from the other side of the mattress rumbled overhead, and London's eyes widened. "What is all that racket?"

A well-muscled arm reached for me but found Ralph instead. Ralph licked it too.

"Ralph!" Romeo grumped.

London laughed, bouncing on her feet beside the bed.

Romeo propped himself up, peering over my body to look at our daughter. "What are you laughing at?" he asked, arching a blond brow.

"Daddy got dog drool!"

"Oh, you think that's funny?" he mused and shot up.

She squealed, but my football player husband was

nothing if not athletic, and he snatched her up, lifting her over me and into the bed. His defined arms held her up in the air even as his back hit the blankets.

London laughed, kicking her feet in the air as her bedhead hung around her face, concealing her smile but not her laughter.

"Daddy!"

Romeo roared and tossed her up. She squealed, and he caught her, holding her in the air some more. The bunny dangled between them, one of its ears pooling in the center of Romeo's bare chest.

Roscoe barked and shoved his head in the space between Romeo and his daughter, then barked again. I laughed.

"Help, Roscoe! Help!" London yelled.

He barked more. The other three dogs bounded back on the bed, trampling us and joining in the chaos. Romeo ordered them off the bed, and as soon as they were gone, London kicked her feet.

"Again!" she demanded.

Romeo tossed her up into the air again, and my heart leaped into my throat. It didn't matter how many times I'd seen him do this; it always made me nervous. But he caught her just like he always did and pulled London down into a hug. His hand got lost in her wild mane, and he pressed a kiss to the top of her head. "Good morning, strawberry."

He'd been calling her that since I was pregnant and craved strawberry milkshakes constantly. After she was born, the nickname continued, and now I knew she would forever be Romeo's strawberry.

"It's pancake Sunday!" she declared, her dark head popping up from his shoulder.

"Yeah? Well, I'm too hungry to wait for pancakes," he announced and rolled, tickling her stomach. "I'm gonna eat you instead!"

She laughed and hollered when he buried his face in her stomach and blew out a breath, making a horrible fart sound.

"What is going on in here?" Blue demanded from the doorway. His blond hair was sticking up on one side, and he was rubbing the sleep from his face.

"Blue! Help me!"

Ever loyal to his little sister, Blue launched himself onto the bed to tackle Romeo. The three of them got into some kind of wrestling match while the dogs barked and ran around the room.

This house was completely unruly.

I loved it so much.

Asher appeared, his blond head streaking by the foot of the bed. Not quite as big as his brother, he had to climb onto the mattress, plopping himself in my lap and then scrambling in front of me.

He held his arms out to his sides like a little shield. "I'll protect you, Mom."

"My hero." I ran a hand through his blond locks. He was the only one of my children that didn't wake up with wild bedhead every morning.

My protection lasted all of three seconds before Romeo reached out and snatched him away so he could tickle him too.

A pillow went flying, and I narrowly missed a little foot to my face. "I haven't even had my coffee yet, Roman Anderson."

"Uh-oh," Romeo told the kids. "Mommy feels left out."

I shook my head adamantly. "N—"

I was dragged into the foray as little fingers came from every direction to tickle me. Thankfully, it only lasted a moment before I was tucked beneath my husband's large body as he planted himself over me, his arms on either side of my head.

"That's enough," he mused. "Your mother is prone to injury."

"I am not!" I hollered, indignant.

"Yes, you are!" all three of my traitorous children answered.

I gasped. "Roman Anderson, did you teach them that?"

"Now, smalls, you know I'd never."

I harumphed. After ten years, his charm didn't work on me.

Romeo nuzzled his face against my cheek. The blond scruff on his jaw tickled the corner of my lips. "I told them you were the most precious thing and we had to protect you at all costs."

Fine.

His charm still worked on me. Every. Single. Time.

"Romeo." I sighed.

He dipped his head, and my fingers pushed into the hair at the nape of his neck.

"Ew!" the boys yelled.

His rumbling laughter vibrated his lips against mine. I felt his growing erection against my hip, and I opened my eyes, meeting the ones already staring into mine. Even after all these years, chemistry swirled between us. The want I had for him never waned.

"I'm hungry," Ash announced.

"Me too," Romeo echoed, a familiar dark glint in his eyes.

"I guess I can't cancel pancake Sunday after all," I told the room.

"It's tradition," Blue stated.

"You're right, son. It's a family tradition," Romeo replied.

"Why don't you go see if Jax and Nova are up and meet me down in the kitchen?"

The boys leaped off the bed and ran for the door, the dogs hot on their heels.

London stood on the edge of the bed, bunny at her side as she judged the distance to the floor. "Daddy..."

Romeo was up and over the side of the bed in no time, grabbing her up and swinging her to the floor. The second her feet touched down, she was running off after her brothers.

Romeo turned back, his eyes drifting over my body still lying in bed. Holding my stare, he leaned forward, shoving his arm under the covers to wrap his hand around my ankle. Dragging me across the mattress, he made it so my legs were hanging off the side and he was wedged between them.

He was coming up on his ten-year anniversary of playing in the NFL. Most quarterbacks didn't last this long, but Romeo was an exception. He was considered one of the greatest quarterbacks in history and *the* best in Maryland Knight history. His body was still honed and lithe, his skill and experience making him even more of a powerhouse on the field.

"Where were we?" he murmured, coming over me so we were chest to chest.

My legs wrapped around his waist, and he shifted, pressing his cock against my core. Tingles of awareness shot through me, my toes curling in as my body responded to him the way it always had.

"I'm supposed to be making pancakes."

His hand pushed between the back of my head and the mattress, cradling me in his palm as his mouth swept against mine. I forgot about breakfast. The noise of the kids down the hall muted, and my lips parted on a sigh. Our tongues tangled, stroking against each other languidly, stealing a moment in time when only the two of us existed.

Even though my eyes were closed, my world was alight with color, the love between us so vibrant it was never really dark.

I arched, back lifting off the mattress as I wrapped my arms around his neck, pressing closer. Under the tank top I wore, my nipples turned sensitive as I rubbed them against his hard chest. A garbled sound rumbled deep in his throat, and his hips thrust, making me gasp.

He was so hard that if the clothes weren't between us, he would already be inside me. As it was, the shorts I wore were damp, and I wiggled against them, wanting them out of the way.

Ripping my mouth from his, I pressed my face into his neck. "*Romeo.*"

The muscles in his back rippled. Against me, his abs flexed when he lifted me off the bed and carried me into the bathroom. He kicked the door closed, then turned to lock it, pressing my back against the door and kissing me once more.

Bold, I rocked against him while dipping my fingers into the waistband of his boxer briefs. He pulled back suddenly, eyes like blue flames, the tops of his cheekbones flushed.

I leaned in, fusing our mouths together again, and our tongues lashed together, more aggressively this time as he walked backward to reach into the shower and turn it on.

When he didn't step inside, I paused, and he pinned me against the bathroom door once more. "Hopefully, it will cover the sound you make when you moan my name." Holding me with one arm, he shoved his boxers down with the other.

"Are you gonna moan for me, baby? Hm?" he asked, nibbling on my lip as he spoke. "I want to hear you say my name."

"Romeo," I said, chasing his lips for more.

He didn't even bother pulling down my shorts. Instead, he dragged the crotch to the side and pushed his hot, pulsing head inside me.

As he wished, I moaned, tingles racing over my entire body as my arms went slack around his shoulders. My head hit the door as I sighed, wiggling and trying to sink farther onto his length.

A firm hand grasped my chin, pulling my face down. Everything was slightly out of focus but not because my glasses were still on the nightstand. Romeo had the power to blur everything else.

"I love you," he said, the blue fire in his stare burning me to the core. "There will never be a love like ours ever again."

He thrust up, punctuating his words by claiming me completely. He was so deep it almost created an ache, but before I could think about it, he pulled out and thrust back in. My body slid up the door, and I moaned again.

"Hold on to me, Rim. Hold on and don't let go."

I fell into his chest, locking my thighs and arms around him as tight as I could. Pressing my lips against his ear, I whispered, *"I love you."*

He started to move then, pumping into my body like a man with only one goal. My fingers dug into the firm muscles of his shoulders, anchoring myself as my body tightened until I felt like a band with no more give, ready to snap.

I made a light sound, and he growled in response. "You know what I want."

"Please, Romeo," I pleaded. *"Romeo."*

His dick swelled inside me, pulsing as my body stretched to accommodate his domination. Grasping my hips, he pulled me down at the same time he thrust up, and I burst apart right there in his arms.

Ecstasy stole everything for long moments, and when I came back, my cheek was pillowed on his shoulders, sweat smeared his chest, and light aftershocks still rippled his abs.

I didn't know how he held me up so long, but we stayed as we were, his cock buried inside me until our breathing returned to normal and there was a small knock on the other side of the bathroom door.

"Mommy!" London called. "We want pancakes."

"Mommy will be there in a minute," Romeo called. "She's washing off the dog drool."

London laughed, her feet pounding as she ran from the bedroom.

I lifted my head to meet his stare, both of us smiling.

2

Romeo

THE SCENT OF BACON SATURATED THE KITCHEN, MINGLING with the slightly nutty brown butter aroma from the pile of pancakes Rimmel was making at the stove.

"That should be enough to feed all of you," she said, sliding the last perfectly round, golden, and fluffy concoction onto a massive white platter. Over the years, she'd become an expert at making them, and I'd argue to the grave that no one made a pancake better than my wife.

"Will you take that to the table for me?" she asked, turning toward me, an oversized spatula in her hand, flour in her hair, and batter smeared on her glasses.

Yeah, my girl was hella good at making up a pancake, but she was still a hot mess. Chuckling, I palmed her waist, rubbing where it dipped in at the side. Her bare toes bumped my feet when I moved closer, and she tipped her chin up to look at me.

Tugging the glasses off her face, I mused, "How do you even see out of these smudged things?"

"Mostly, I squint." She informed me, demonstrating exactly how she did so by scrunching up her nose and narrowing her brown eyes. "Plus, I could probably make pancakes in my sleep at this point."

"Oh hells no!" Braeden erupted, coming into the kitchen behind us. "Don't even think about it, tutor girl. You'll burn the place down."

Rim snorted, and I suppressed a smile. "Not even I'm that clumsy, Braeden James."

Braeden stopped halfway to the coffee maker. "Tell her, Rome."

"You're on your own, man," I said, using the hem of my shirt to clean sticky pancake batter off her lenses.

A dark brow arched halfway up his forehead. "Need I remind you of just last month when you sat down on the bench in the hallway to put on your shoes and the entire thing flipped on its side, leaving you covered in bruises for a week?"

I grimaced, recalling that particular phone call. I'd been out of town for training, and Blue called to tell me his mother was holding ice on her hip.

"Or that time you got lost on a mountain at Bearpaw and broke your ankle." Braeden went on. "Or last year when you tripped over the dog and—"

Rimmel groaned. "You made your point."

"I love ya, sis, but you're a walking disaster," Braeden said, coming over to ruffle her wild mane of hair.

A cloud of flour puffed out around his hand, and he coughed. "I'm gonna suffocate!"

Rimmel smacked him in the stomach with the spatula, and bits of pancake batter smeared his T-shirt. He grabbed the utensil and tossed it into the sink. "You better get your girl, Rome."

"Carry those into the dining room," Rimmel ordered, and he grabbed the large platter obediently.

A dark-headed streak shot into the room between us, a hand reaching up to steal a pancake off the plate. "Thanks, Dad!" Jax hollered as he darted for the door.

"Go sit at the table," Rimmel called after him.

"He's a growing boy. He's hungry." Braeden defended.

"Take that too," Rimmel commanded, pointing at the platter of bacon.

"Am I your brother or your servant?" he muttered.

"BBFL," Rimmel countered.

Yep. They still said that.

"You're lucky I love ya."

Braeden carried the food into the adjoining dining room, and I slid the clean glasses onto Rimmel's face.

"I love you most," I told her, leaning down to kiss her nose.

Stretching up on her toes, she draped her arms over my shoulders and pecked my lips.

The back door burst open, and the sound of feet slapping the floor stole our attention. "Uncle Romeo!"

I turned just in time to catch Andi who'd launched herself at me without any warning. A few steps behind, Drew made a pained sound, but I caught her midair and lifted her over my head. She squealed just like my daughter had earlier that morning.

Her pin-straight black hair waved around her face as she laughed. "How'd you get in here?" I asked, then announced over my shoulder, "Rim, we have an intruder!"

Andi laughed. "I live here!"

I shook my head. "Nope. The girl who lives here is nothing but a little peanut. You're too big to be her."

"It's me, Uncle Romeo! I got big while you were gone."

I didn't bother telling her I'd only been gone two weeks. To her, it probably felt like longer. Hell, sometimes it felt like years to me. Holding her out, I squinted at her. "Andi, is that you?"

She laughed and nodded.

I pulled her in and kissed her cheek. "What have your daddies been feeding you?"

"French fries!"

I laughed.

"Andi!" London called, racing in from the other room, three dogs on her trail. "Come sit by me."

Andi wiggled, and I put her down. The girls raced off.

"Be careful," Trent called after them as they raced by. Beside him, Drew shook his head.

"I'll watch her," Travis said, appearing from behind Trent, his dark eyes already tracking where the girls had gone.

"Hey, Trav," I said, holding out my fist.

Travis smashed his against it. "Hi, Uncle Romeo."

"You ready for the game later?"

One thing that sucked most about football season was being gone for the boys' games. Blue, Jax, Travis, and Asher all played football. We went to as many games and practices as we could, but me and B missed more than we wanted. It was one of the reasons we were home this weekend. It was a short trip, but we weren't playing because we'd just had a Thursday game. The boys' games got rained out yesterday, so they were happening today, which meant we could watch them.

Travis nodded.

"Come on. Let's go eat before it gets cold," Rimmel said, shooing us all toward the dining room.

"Did you get into a fight with a bag of flour, sis?" Trent mused.

"You try cooking for seven children," Rimmel retorted.

"Eleven, if you ask me," Ivy mused, strolling past the island to grab a pitcher of orange juice from the fridge.

Her blond hair hung past her shoulders in loose waves, and even though it was early, she was fashionably dressed in loose green-and-pink striped pants and a matching striped sweater. Overtop, she layered several golden necklaces, and her nails were bright pink. Beneath the wide hem of the pants, a pair of brown slippers stuck out.

Rimmel laughed. "That's the truth." She agreed and grabbed a basket of muffins, tucking them into her chest.

The girls went ahead, leaving me, Trent, and Drew staring at each other.

"Did they just call us children?" Drew mused.

"They're the ones that need a babysitter," Trent quipped as we moved into the full dining room.

All seven kids were already around the large wooden table. There were dogs beneath the large wooden surface and a couple squished between the chairs as they waited patiently for whatever food the kids might drop.

London leaned across the table and snatched a piece of bacon, but instead of eating it, she handed it off to Ralph who was right there waiting.

"I saw that," I told her.

"But, Daddy, he's hungry," she said, batting those baby blues at me.

Rimmel told me all the time that my eyes had an effect, but I never understood until my daughter used them against me.

I leaned over her, bracing my arm on the back of her chair. "I'm hungry too."

She laughed, crawling over the table again to grab another piece and push it into my open mouth.

"Mmm," I said, chewing loudly. "Thanks, strawberry," I said, smacking a greasy kiss to her cheek.

"Eww, Daddy!"

"Sit by me, Dad!" Ash called, patting an empty chair beside him. I slid into it as everyone descended on the massive spread of food the girls put out.

I mostly stuck to eggs with bacon and some fruit but did indulge in one of my wife's pancakes with some maple syrup.

"You boys ready for the game later?" I asked.

Asher nodded enthusiastically. "Blue is gonna start today."

Surprised, I glanced at my oldest son. "You're starting today?"

He nodded.

A grin cracked my face, and I abandoned my food to lean around Ash and hug my son. "That's awesome, Blue-Jay. You worked hard. I'm so proud of you."

"Thanks, Dad."

He didn't seem nearly as excited as I expected, and I pulled back a little to look at him. "Are you nervous?"

He shrugged.

"Why didn't you tell me?" I asked gently.

"I was going to."

I glanced at Rim, and she gave me a curious look, frowning slightly. I turned back to our son. "We can go outside after breakfast and throw the ball around for a while if you want. Warm up your arm."

"Can I come too?" Asher asked.

"Of course," I answered.

"Me too," Jax put in.

"Me too!" Andi yelled.

"You're too little to play football with these guys," Travis told her.

"Am not!"

"You'll get squished."

"Daddy," Andi wailed.

"I'm sure Trav can throw the ball with you for a little while," Trent reasoned, glancing at Travis.

Travis sighed. "Fine."

"How about it, son? Want to toss the ball?" I asked Blue.

"Sure," he replied and stuffed a big bite of pancakes between his lips.

I let him eat while everyone chattered around us, but I couldn't shake the feeling something wasn't quite right.

3

After breakfast was cleaned up, I shut myself in the bathroom for a much-needed shower. Between the dog drool, my extracurricular activities with Romeo this morning, and then cooking up a storm in the kitchen, I was less than fresh.

I loved it, though. Having such a big, rambunctious family was literally a dream come true. This weekend felt a little extra special because Romeo was home. Now that the season was really in full swing, I knew his time off would be much less.

After a thorough wash, I stepped out of the steamy shower with a towel wrapped around my body and worked some leave-in conditioner through my damp strands. My hair wasn't as long as it used to be. With three kids and the animal shelter, it was too much to fight with, and I'd had it cut to a length just below my shoulders. It was still long enough to pull up but required a lot less brushing.

After getting it detangled and smoothing on my skin care, I padded into the closet off the bathroom and switched on the light.

Romeo's Alpha U hoodie was covered in flour and pancake batter from earlier, so that was out. Even after ten years, it was still my favorite thing to wear. It was a little worn these days and maybe had a hole or two, but I didn't care. I loved that hoodie and planned to wear until it disintegrated right off my body.

I glanced at the purple Knights hoodie with his name on the back but decided to try wearing something a little different since we had two games later. I found that wearing my husband's name to the kids' football or even school events got a lot of mixed reactions. Some people would fall over themselves to be overly nice and accommodating while others made snide comments and drilled dirty looks into the back of my head.

FYI, dirty looks could be felt. Frankly, they gave me a headache.

It was the price we paid for "fame," even if we did live on the other side of the state from the Knights home base. When the boys started school, we'd been faced with the decision of putting them in private or letting them go to the same public school Romeo and Braeden had gone to.

In the end, we figured it probably wouldn't be much different either place because everyone knew Romeo and Braeden. Romeo and I would still be the "royal" couple of the NFL no matter what school they attended. So we chose the public school.

Overall, it seemed a good choice. We wanted the boys to have as much of a normal upbringing as possible and tried to keep them out of the spotlight and in a regular routine. Yes, our house was hidden behind a wall and gate, but we still did playdates and encouraged them to join clubs and play sports.

There had been a handful of times people wanted to do playdates with them when they were small just so they could get an invite to the compound and see behind the walls. One bad experience with Nova was all it took, and we decided play dates would have to be held elsewhere.

After pulling on a pair of loose-fit jeans and some socks, I reached for a snug, white long-sleeved T-shirt. I was partway through drying my hair when London skipped into the bathroom, Betty still clutched in her arms. Instead of pajamas, she was wearing a pair of blue overalls, a shirt with stars all over it beneath it.

"Murphy," she called, going to the corner where my one-eyed black cat lay in a fluffy bed. After the arrival of our three children and numerous dogs, he started hanging out in our bathroom and master closet when he needed some peace and quiet, so I'd moved in a bed for him.

He was roughly thirteen now, but he was still healthy and enjoying life. He still sauntered into the kitchen every morning for his treats and curled up in my lap when I read.

London laid her bunny in the bed with Murphy and plopped down beside him to pet his head. His one eye blinked up at her, and his tail swished. The running hairdryer muffled my laugh as I watched him resign himself to having his nap interrupted.

After petting him, London moved her bunny closer, laying it right up against his black fur. Murphy laid his head back down and closed his eye. Seconds later, London was bounding out of the bathroom only to return a moment later with a small blanket.

I shut off the dryer and set it aside, watching her through the mirror as she covered her cat and bunny.

"Was he cold?" I asked.

"He's old. He needs extra cover on his bones."

I laughed. "Well, he seems to like it," I observed, noting his excessively loud purring.

"He sounds like Uncle Drew's fastback," London said, patting his back.

"I think you're right," I said. "Want me to braid your hair?"

"Sure," she said, leaving Betty with Murphy and coming over to where I stood at the counter.

I lifted her, groaning like she was too heavy, and sat her on the counter. She scooted back and turned so she was facing the mirror, tucking her feet beneath her.

"Combing your hair is a lot of work," she said seriously.

I nodded. "You're right it is."

I began working the brush through her tangled strands. Her dark hair went partway down her back. "Are the boys outside playing football?"

She nodded. "Andi too." Her little nose wrinkled. "I don't want to play football."

Poor Romeo. From the day she was born, he'd hoped his daughter would get his athleticism, but the only things she'd gotten from him were her blue eyes and charm. The rest of her was all me.

"You can do whatever you want to do," I told her. "Be whatever you want."

"I want to color!"

"Hold still first so I can finish your hair."

"It's taking too long."

I laughed and quickly finished up the single braid and tied it with a blue tie. "Ta-da!"

"Thanks, Mom!"

She went to jump off the counter, but I caught her. "Be careful."

"I have nine lives like Murphy."

"Better not tell your daddy that."

She ran for the door.

"What about Betty?" I called after her.

"She's hanging with Murphy."

I glanced at the cat, and he turned his one eye toward me. I bent down to stroke his soft fur. "Good boy, Murph. You're a patient one."

He purred loudly, and I smiled.

Somewhere in the house, a door slammed. Footsteps pounding on the stairs had me going through the bedroom.

"Blue," Romeo called as a little blond-headed blur rushed past me.

"Blue-Jay?"

My son didn't answer as he rushed into his bedroom and slammed the door.

I blinked and started after him, but a gentle hand curled around my wrist, stopping me. I turned back. "Romeo?"

"Let me," he said.

"What's wrong?" I asked.

"Let me," he repeated.

I nodded. If Romeo wanted to talk to his son, then I would never get in his way. He was a good father, and our kids were insanely lucky to have him.

"Go," I said softly, stepping back so he could get by.

Romeo moved past but then stopped, reaching back to pull me into his side. "Love you, smalls."

I smiled. "Love you too," I whispered. "Now go talk to Blue."

He pecked a kiss on my forehead and then went swiftly to the door, knocking softly. "It's Dad. Can I come in?"

"Go away!"

Romeo turned the knob and pushed open the door. "You know I can't do that." And then he stepped inside, gently closing the door behind him.

4

____

The sky was bright and blue, but the ground was slightly squishy from the rainstorm the day before. The air was crisp, edging to cold when the wind blew. All six kids hopped around on the grass, not one of them standing still.

The only one not out here was my daughter who seemed to care as much about football and playing in the mud as her mother—which was not at all.

Nova had no interest in playing either, but she did like to stand along the sidelines and shake the purple and gold pompoms Braeden had swiped from one of the Knights cheerleaders.

Swiped = charmed her into handing them over.

He probably would have brought home a uniform too if it wouldn't have been too big on his ten-year-old daughter. Amen for that. My niece didn't need to be running around here in a tiny skirt.

Thank God London stayed inside. With pants on.

"Throw it to me, Uncle Romeo!" Andi called, jumping around and waving her arms. The football was practically the same size as her. But she was too cute to deny.

"Hold your arms out," I told her. "Get ready."

She planted her little feet into the grass, mud splashing on her ankles. Gently, I tossed the ball, and she squealed as it came at her.

It hit her arms and bounced out, but she chased after it, scooping it back up against her chest. "I got it!"

"And I got you!" Braeden roared, rushing up behind her and lifting her into the air.

She shrieked and giggled.

Braeden tucked her and the football under his arm and ran with her. "Touchdown!" he hollered, plunking her down on the ground.

Nova cheered, and Andi tossed the ball down, a peanut's version of a spike. "Daddy, I scored!"

Trent and Drew both clapped and whistled.

Andi started forward, but her foot was stuck in the mud. I watched her tug it out, a loud sucking sound swallowing her sneaker. "I'm stuck!" she yelled, trying to lift her leg again.

"Daddy!" she wailed.

Travis appeared and lifted her off her feet. She wrapped her muddy legs around him, smearing him with dirt. "Sisters," he muttered, hauling her over to the side by Nova.

She busied herself with Nova and the pompoms while the four boys spread out in the grass with me, Braeden, Trent, and Drew.

We tossed the ball around a bit, letting each boy catch a few passes and run a few. Blue hung back a little more than usual, and it confirmed for me that something was definitely up.

I caught a pass from Trent and turned to my oldest son.

"How about you toss me a few? Let's get your arm warmed up for later."

We never expected the boys to play football. Sure, I hoped they would. With me and B in the NFL and Trent who played through college, sharing our love for the sport with our kids was something we all looked forward to.

Still, if any of them had shown no interest, we wouldn't have pushed it on them. We wanted our kids to be who they wanted to be and not who *we* wanted.

All four boys took a liking to it. I suspected Asher wanted to be like his big brothers, Blue and Jax, but he seemed to have fun when playing. For Trav, it was a good energy outlet and good for team building (sometimes he was a bit of a loner).

Blue nodded and rubbed a hand over his messy blond hair as he took the ball and walked away. I glanced at B, wondering if he also thought Blue seemed a little apprehensive. Braeden gestured at me with his chin, an acknowledgment that he sensed it too.

Trent jogged toward Blue, a basket of footballs in his hands, and set them at his side. He said something I couldn't hear that got a small smile from my son, and then he gave his shoulder a pat and jogged toward the rest of us so he could catch a pass.

"Go, Blue-Jay!" Nova cheered from the side, with Andi echoing her words.

Blue palmed the ball, lining his fingers along the laces just like I taught him. His first pass was a little wobbly but made it into Jax's hands.

Then he tossed to Asher.

"Right here," I called, holding out my hands.

He hesitated, then pulled back and launched the ball. It fell a little short, and I lunged forward to catch it with the tips of my fingers.

"Good throw," I said, straightening up. "Next time—"

"I'll never be as good as you!" Blue burst out. Then he grabbed another ball and spiked it into the dirt before taking off in the direction of the house.

A beat of shock rippled over me as I watched him haul ass away. "Blue!"

He kept running, not even looking back.

"Is eight years old too young for imposter syndrome?" Braeden wondered, stepping up beside me.

The breath whooshed out of him when I slammed the football into his middle. "I'm going."

"Was just a theory," B wheezed as I jogged after my son.

As loath as I was to admit it, B's theory had some weight to it.

And that pissed me off.

Blue was halfway up the stairs when I rounded the corner. I called out for him, but he just kept going.

Upstairs, Rimmel was in the hallway, brown eyes wide and concerned behind her glasses. "What's wrong?"

"Let me," I said, frustration and maybe even a little shame tightening my chest.

"Go," she said, stepping back so I could follow our son.

Her confidence and infallible trust in me and my ability as a father shone in her eyes, and I reached for it and held on. I might be an alpha. I might be the backbone of this family… but being a parent was hard. I wasn't so cocky that I thought I knew how to fix everything. Especially when I was the one who likely caused the problem.

But Rim loved me anyway. "Love you, smalls," I told her, the words unable to express everything I felt for her.

Her smile was encouraging, the sheen in her eyes holding a note of understanding. I couldn't do life without her.

After pressing those feelings against her head with my

lips, I knocked on our son's bedroom door. "It's Dad. Can I come in?"

"Go away!"

"You know I can't do that," I said and slipped into the room.

It didn't seem that long ago when the room was just a nursery with a crib and rocking chair. But here I was, eight years later, and the room was completely different. There was a full-sized bed upholstered in dark-gray fabric with built-in LED lighting that lit up the headboard and footboard in neon blue. At the very top of the headboard was a charging station where he plugged in his iPad and handheld game. Our kids didn't have phones yet. The press still loved my family, and while they weren't as vicious as when he was born, they were still far too interested in using us as headlines. We all agreed we'd keep our kids off the internet for as long as we could.

On either side of the bed were nightstands, and beneath it was a rug that was thick and soft underfoot. There was large basket for toys, a small basketball hoop on the wall, and a bookshelf that held more Legos than books.

He wasn't on the bed but across from it, hiding in a chair that was more of a swing suspended from the ceiling. The bottom of it was lined with more blue LED lights that made it look like some kind of floating pod.

It swung lightly from when he'd thrown himself inside, but I didn't go over to it, just let him hide in the fabric making up the swing.

Leaning against the bedroom door, I tried to relax as I looked at the letters spelling his name across the far wall.

"Want to tell me what happened?" I asked.

Silence.

"Okay, I'll guess," I said conversationally.

"You're nervous about starting today."

Silence.

"You're worried the mud was gonna eat your leg like it did Andi's."

A light giggle.

"You don't want to play football anymore."

Silence.

I sighed and pushed off the wall, going over to sit in front of the swing. From my position on my ass, I was slightly lower than him but could see into the wide opening. It was shadowed inside, so I couldn't make out his face, which was also downturned to his lap.

"I'm sorry, son."

His chin lifted, his blue eyes wide with surprise.

I nodded. "Maybe you feel like I expect you to play football because I do. I'm sorry if I ever made you feel pressured. If you don't want to play, if it's not fun and something you love, then you don't have to do it. I won't be mad. Mom won't be mad. No one will be mad. We just want you to be happy."

He didn't say anything, and I felt like I was swallowing rocks. Like I was somehow failing him. I never wanted to be that dad, the kind who put weight on their kids' shoulders to be people they weren't. Even still…

I cleared my throat. "You definitely don't have to play, but it's important you go to today's game. Finish out the season. You made a commitment to your team and told them you'd be there. A good person honors their commitments. If you don't want to start, we can tell Coach and—"

"They said I'm not good enough to start and the only reason I am is because of you!" Blue wailed, leaning forward to stick his blond head out of the swing.

The muscles in the back of my neck corded, and a gust of anger blew through me. "Who said that?"

"RJ and Lincoln."

I told myself it was wrong to have bad thoughts about eight-year-old boys. Even if they did say asshole things to my kid. Weren't they too young for this?

I blew out a breath. "When did they say this?"

"When Coach told us at practice that I was starting." He paused. "RJ's dad seemed mad."

My eyes whipped up. "Did he say something to you?"

He shook his head.

My eyes narrowed. "To your mom?"

He shook his head again. "She was sitting with Uncle Trent."

I made a sound and tried to calm the protective instincts stirring inside me. I was grateful to Trent and Drew for watching out for the fam when B and I were on the road, but it was hard sometimes. I wanted to be the one here.

"RJ started last game?" I asked, steering back to the conversation while trying to remember the video clips Rim had sent while I'd been on the road. Truth was I didn't pay much attention to the kids that weren't ours.

"He's a year older than me," Blue said as if an entire year seemed like such a big gap. "And he said I suck and throw like a girl."

"You don't say suck," I intoned, practically hearing Rimmel gasp in the back of my head. "Teammates support each other, not break each other down. And you don't throw like a girl. Even if you did, girls are cool."

"I don't throw as good as you."

My chest constricted. Reaching into the swing, I tugged him out and into my lap. "I've had lots of years of practice. Lots of coaching and training. There were times when I wasn't so good."

"Really?" he asked, dipping his head back to look at me.

I nodded. "For sure. I didn't always start. The first few

years I played, I sat on the bench more than I was on the field."

He giggled. "No you didn't!"

I nodded sagely. "Ask Grandma. I used to hand out Gatorade to the players who got to play."

He laughed again.

"You laughing at me?" I mused. When his giggles died away, I said, "And then in college, I fell and broke my arm. We didn't even know if I'd be able to play again."

"You broke your arm?"

I nodded. "It was scary. I couldn't play for a long time. Almost missed my shot in the NFL."

"But you didn't."

"No, I practiced even more. I went to therapy and taught myself to throw with my other arm."

"Is that why they call you am-bed-ectris?"

"Ambidextrous," I corrected. "How do you know they call me that?"

"I hear the announcers say it."

"Right." Sometimes I forgot just how spongelike kids were, learning and absorbing everything. "I wasn't always the best," I told him. "And I'm still not. I have bad games. Bad throws. But I keep trying." Blue settled deeper into my lap, so I kept talking. "Some kids—some people," I corrected, thinking of the parents. "They're gonna be jealous and say bad shit."

"Ahh, you said sh—"

"Don't repeat that. And don't tell your mother," I interrupted. "Some people are gonna say things that hurt, but just because they hurt, it doesn't mean they're true."

"But my throws out there were bad."

"They weren't bad. You're a good player. You have good instincts, and you're a natural leader."

"I am?"

"Definitely. That's why Coach wants to try you out in the starter position. And maybe next week, he'll give someone else a shot, and that's okay. You're young, play all the positions. See what you like best. Have fun."

He nodded.

"And if you decide playing football isn't fun, then you don't have to play. I'm proud of you no matter what."

"I want to play," he told me.

"You sure?" I eyed him. "Maybe you want to drag home dogs like your mom."

Blue laughed.

"Or maybe you want to do math, read books, or be a cheerleader."

"A cheerleader?" he questioned.

"Nova seems to like those pompoms. Maybe you would too."

"Daaad," he groaned.

"I'm just saying," I teased. "Whatever you like is okay with me."

"I like football. I want to be like you."

Pride swelled in my chest. It took a moment for me to find my voice. Rubbing my hand over his hair, I said, "Just be yourself, Blue-Jay."

"Can we go play now?" he asked.

Another thing I often forgot about with kids. They bounced back faster than a rubber band. "Sure."

He scrambled up, but I grabbed him around the waist and pulled him back down, hugging him tight. "I love you, son."

"Love you too, dad."

"The next time someone gives you a hard time, tell me. Even if I'm not home, you can call. And if you don't want to talk to me, you have a whole house full of people who love you and want to listen."

"Okay."

"Except Ralph. Pretty sure he's hard of hearing. He never listens to a word I say."

"He listens to Mom!"

"Well, your mother is prettier than me."

"Come on. Let's go play!" He raced from the room as fast as he'd raced into it.

I got to my feet and blew out a breath.

Rimmel appeared in the doorway, a soft smile on her lips.

"You eavesdropping on my talk with our son, smalls?"

"I'm so thankful the dean forced me to tutor you all those years ago," she mused.

I laughed and caught her around the waist, pulling her close. "Guess it's a good thing I was failing."

"You were good with him."

I buried my face in her hair, inhaling her familiar scent. "I don't want our kids to be hurt for my fame."

"They won't."

I pulled back, searching her face. "You have. More than once."

"That makes me an expert," she said, pushing the glasses up her nose. "And I'm telling you having your love overshadows, outshines, and beats out any amount of hate thrown my way. It's the same for our kids. We're all so lucky to have you."

"Haters gonna hate," I quipped.

"Posers gonna pose," she countered.

I grinned over her head. "Lovers gonna love."

"Well, I definitely love you."

I leaned down to capture her mouth.

"Dad! Come on!" Blue hollered from somewhere in the house.

I groaned, and Rimmel pulled away, laughing. "Better get going," she said, going ahead of me from the room.

"Rim."

She glanced over her shoulder. "Rome."

I muffled a grin. What a brat. "I don't need to tell you to stay the hell away from that RJ's dad, right?"

She pursed her lips. "I'm perfectly capable of handling—"

"Rimmel Anderson."

She sighed. "Well, I'm certainly not going to go to my son's football game and start a fight."

"Well, I will if you don't keep away from the bastard."

"I'll stay away from him." She promised, and I felt better.

For two seconds.

"Unless, of course, I see him near my children. If that happens, I make no promises."

"Deal," I said, knowing I'd never get her to agree to anything less. I'd have to warn Trent and Drew.

Another twinge of guilt—jealousy? wistfulness?—rolled through me at the thought of having my brothers watching out for my wife.

"Romeo?" Rimmel's voice was soft just like the footsteps that brought her to my side. "What's the matter?"

"Sometimes I wonder if playing ball costs too much."

She gasped, surprise flashing across her features.

"Do you think I spend too much time away?"

She stretched onto her tiptoes to grab my face and pull it down. Holding it firmly, she stared into my eyes. "Football is a part of you. Playing makes you happy. I want you to be happy. You don't have to choose. You can have it all."

I opened my mouth, but she squeezed my cheeks and kept going. "And when football doesn't make you happy anymore, that's when you walk away. But no matter what, I'm proud of you, Roman Anderson."

"That's what I told Blue."

"I know. I was eavesdropping."

I threw back my head and laughed. Reaching down, I lifted her off her feet, her legs winding around my waist.

"I'd like to try for a few more years," I confessed. It was something I hadn't ever said out loud before. "I always kinda thought fifteen years would be my sweet spot. Long enough to leave a legacy but short enough that I can go out at the top."

Rimmel smiled, rubbing her palms over my unshaven jaw. "Sounds good to me."

"Really?"

She nodded.

I pressed my forehead against hers. "You're my favorite."

"I know."

5

PANCAKE SUNDAY WAS A THING IN THIS FAMILY, BUT SO WAS football Sunday. Especially when Romeo and Braeden were at away games and we couldn't be there to support them.

I still loved going to Romeo's games, but all the kids except Andi were in school this year. That made traveling hard because we liked to stick to somewhat of a routine with them. With London in kindergarten, Asher in second grade, and Blue in third, it was quite busy.

The Knights were playing in Buffalo this weekend, and snow was blowing around the field as the game went on. We all watched via the large screen in the living room, the coffee table covered in snacks and drinks. Blankets covered the couches and chairs, and bean bags dotted the floor.

"This has been a tough game," Ivy murmured. "My stomach is in knots."

I made a sound of agreement. "There does seem to be a

lot of tension on the field." I worried, glancing at the screen and hoping for a shot of my husband.

"It's because the season is winding down. Getting close to the playoffs," Trent explained.

"Daddy!" London yelled, clapping as Romeo flashed onscreen. He was on the sidelines with a large coat wrapped around him. He was talking with the coach, nodding at something the man was saying from behind his clipboard.

"There he is." I agreed, drinking in the sight of him. It felt like forever since I'd seen him last.

"Does anyone want anything from the kitchen?" Drew asked, heading behind the couch.

"No thanks," I called as the players ran out on the field.

"I need help, Mommy," Asher said, coming over to hand me a pack of fruit snacks that he was struggling to open.

I reached for them, glancing down to rip the top.

Ivy gasped. "No." The protest ripped out of her in such a painful way my head snapped up.

I stared at the screen, noting the way people were converging on a player on the field.

"Drew!" Ivy yelled. "Drew!"

The replay flashed across the screen, which showed Braeden taking a hard hit and going down and several other players landing on top of him.

Gasping, I stood as Drew rushed in from the kitchen.

"Ives?"

She pointed to the TV. "He's not getting up," she croaked.

"What happened to Daddy?" Nova asked, abandoning her toys to stare.

Team doctors and players surrounded Braeden who was still down. My heart started thumping in my throat, stomach twisting as Ivy nearly fell over the coffee table trying to get closer to the TV.

Drew cursed beneath his breath and went to her side,

slipping his arm around his sister's waist. "I'm sure he's fine. Probably just stunned."

"What's stunned?" Jax asked.

"Surprised," Trent explained.

Romeo jogged across the field, everyone cutting a path for him to step right up. As they cleared, we saw Braeden lying on the ground.

A low sob ripped from Ivy.

"Is Daddy hurt?" Nova asked and started to cry.

Romeo moved right in and knelt beside Braeden, his helmet discarded to the side.

Hearing his sister so upset, Jax started to cry too.

Drew picked up Nova, rubbing her back. Jax clutched Ivy, hugging around her waist.

Andi started crying, and Trent picked her up, then moved to my side.

"Why isn't he getting up?" I worried my lower lip.

"They're probably making him lie still." Trent assured us.

"You think so?" Ivy asked, looking over her shoulder. Tears shimmered in her eyes.

"Give them a minute."

A moment later, a cart drove out onto the field, and Romeo lifted Braeden to his feet. Well, foot. All of his weight was balanced on one leg, Braeden's arm draped over Romeo's wide shoulders.

His face was red, but he was alert.

"He's up!" Ivy yelled. "He's up!"

He was loaded onto the cart, legs spread out in front of him. He looked massive and unbreakable sitting there with all his equipment on. But the way they were stabilizing his leg said different.

"He's okay." Ivy assured the kids. "He must have hurt his leg. The doctors will look at him, and he will be okay."

"I want Daddy!" Nova wailed against Drew's shoulder.

"Me too," Jax yelled.

Ivy's eyes found mine, and worry passed between us.

"I'll call Romeo's mother," I said, and not even seconds later, my phone was ringing.

"Valerie," I answered right away.

"We saw. We can be there in twenty minutes," she said instantly.

"You don't mind?"

"Of course not. That's what we do," she said. "Pack a bag. Don't worry about the kids. We'll take care of them."

"Thank you so much."

I ended the call and noticed Ivy had her cell to her ear. When she pulled it away, she said, "Braeden's mom will be here in a few minutes."

Trent glanced up from his phone. "Gamble's sending his plane. It'll be here in two hours."

"I'm going to pack a bag. I'm going to pack something comfortable for Braeden," Ivy told us.

"I'll pack one too." I agreed.

"Where are you going?" Nova wanted to know.

"I'm going to see your daddy. In case he needs a hug."

Her lower lip trembled a bit, and she glanced back at the screen. Braeden had already been taken off the field.

"I want to come too."

"Me too," Jax said.

All the kids started saying they wanted to come.

Ivy's phone started ringing. She nearly dropped it in her haste to answer. "Braeden?" she yelled into the line.

Her shoulders slumped. "Oh, Dr. Brach," she said. It took a moment for her brain to catch up and realize that Dr. Brach was one of the Knights physicians. The second she did, she was white-knuckling the phone. "How is my husband?"

I tripped over my own feet as I rushed to her side, almost falling if Trent hadn't caught me with his free arm.

"Be careful," he warned as I rushed to Ivy.

She angled the phone so I could listen, and we smashed our heads together.

"Mrs. Walker. I have Braeden here. He requested I call you."

Ivy made a sound, and then Braeden's voice filled the line. "Baby."

"Braeden! Oh my god! Are you okay? Are you hurt? You lay there for so long!"

"Breathe," he said, and Ivy sucked in a deep breath.

"You too, sis."

I didn't even question how he knew I was listening; I just did what he said.

"I can't talk long, but I knew you were probably freaking out."

"As we should!" Ivy interrupted. "That was a hard hit. Those players should be punished!"

Braeden laughed, and some of the worst worry coiling in my stomach unclenched. I reached up and grabbed Ivy's wrist, silently offering support.

"I'm fine." He assured her, but he didn't sound as confident and big-headed as usual.

"Don't you lie to us, Braeden James," we both scolded at the same time.

"Tag-teaming me. Damn. A busted knee and a busted ego."

"What's wrong with your knee?" she exclaimed.

"I want my daddy!" Nova cried, rushing over to push between us. "Daddy!"

"The kids saw?" he asked, voice subdued.

"Yes."

"Put me on speaker."

"Are you sure?" Ivy asked, voice trembling.

"I'm sure, baby."

She tapped the screen.

"Hey, munchkins." Braeden's voice filled the room. "I'm just calling to let you know I'm all good. I took a hit, but you know that's part of my job."

"Did you hit your head?" Nova worried.

"No, I was wearing my helmet. I hurt my knee."

"Does it hurt?" Jax asked.

"A little, but I got doc here fixing me up."

"Braeden…" Ivy fretted.

"I gotta go finish up with the doctor, but I wanted you guys to know not to be worried. Don't be scared, okay? I'm good. And I'll call you back later tonight."

After a round of I-love-yous from all the kids, Ivy took the phone off speaker and pushed it to her ear. "I'm coming."

There was a short pause, and she shook her head. "I'm coming, Braeden. Tell me where." After another pause, she said, "We'll be there as soon as we can."

He said something, and her lower lip wobbled. She nodded, then held the phone out to Trent.

He took it. "Hey," he said, then made a bunch of grunts and noises.

I glared at him because it told me nothing. He thought it was funny and winked.

After a moment, he rubbed a hand over his face. "Hang in there."

As he was handing the phone back to Ivy, I snatched it. "I love you, BBFL."

"Back at ya, tutor girl."

"See you soon," I echoed and gave the phone to Ivy.

She said a few more things and then ended the call, dashing the tears from her eyes before they fell.

Forcing a smile, she took in the kids. "See! He's okay."

The kids seemed much better, and I wished it were that easy to feel reassured. I heard the pain masked in my brother's voice, though. I knew he was worse than he let on.

Trent and Drew were having some silent conversation with just their eyes, and my stare went back to the TV, hoping to see Romeo. But the game was over.

"That was fast," I murmured.

"Romeo fired a touchdown into the endzone, and with so little time on the clock left for the other team to catch up, they took a knee on the extra point," Drew explained.

I nodded.

Asher tugged on my hoodie, and I glanced down. "Is Daddy okay?"

I knelt in front of him. "Oh yes, Daddy is fine."

"Who wants a cookie?" Drew asked.

All the kids jumped up and raced into the kitchen.

When they were gone, we looked at Trent.

"They think it's an ACL tear." He informed us.

Ivy pressed a hand over her mouth.

"Possibly a meniscus tear alongside it. But they won't be sure until he gets to the hospital."

The tears Ivy had been holding back fell over, streaking her cheeks. My own eyes welled, threatening to spill over.

"What does that mean exactly, Trent?" I asked, even though I was afraid I knew.

"*If* it's a tear, he's gonna be out the rest of the season. Probably most of next season too."

"He needs surgery," Ivy said.

Trent hesitated. "Probably."

"I'm going to pack," Ivy said, starting to rush from the room.

Trent followed, gently taking her arm and pulling her around. "It's not life-threatening. He's gonna be okay." His voice was gentle.

Ivy melted against Trent's chest, her sob muffled. He

hugged her tight, stroking the back of her blond head. "I can't get the image of him just lying there out of my head," she said.

I nodded, silently agreeing. It was haunting me too.

"C'mon, Ives. Let's go pack," Drew said, appearing to wrap his arm around his sister and direct them to the stairs.

"Can you listen for Romeo's parents?" Drew asked Trent.

"Of course."

"Caroline too," Ivy added, speaking of Braeden's mom.

"I'll let everyone in." Trent promised. "And I'll keep the kids busy."

"I'll help."

We all swung around, surprised to see Travis standing quietly against the wall. His dark eyes were wide, but his face was calm.

"Son," Trent said, going to him. "I thought you were in the kitchen."

He gave a single-shoulder shrug. "I wanted to know about Uncle Braeden."

"Oh, honey," Ivy said, pulling away from Drew to hug her nephew. "He's going to be fine. I'm just worried."

He nodded. "I know."

Trent cupped the back of his head. "It's okay to be worried," he told him. "Being worried about family is natural."

Sometimes Travis had issues expressing his emotions. He bottled up a lot inside. Got angry easily. We knew it was because of the early years of his life. I'd also noticed that my oldest nephew was very empathetic. He felt deeply. It didn't surprise me that he snuck back in here to know the full details about Braeden.

Travis nodded. "He'll be okay, though?" he asked, seeking out Trent for reassurance.

Trent gave it instantly. "Yeah. I talked to him. He just

needs a few X-rays, some ice, and probably surgery, but it's routine. He's healthy and strong. He'll be home by the end of the week."

Travis nodded.

"I really need to go pack." Ivy worried.

"I'll come too." I agreed.

"You want me to hang with you and Dad for a bit?" Drew asked his son.

"I'm good. Go with Aunt Ivy," Travis replied.

"If you need me, I'll be in your aunt's closet." Drew made a face. "If I'm not back in twenty minutes, send a search party."

Travis laughed.

On our way up the stairs, Ivy reached for my hand, and I gave hers a squeeze. It wasn't the first time one of our guys had been injured, but something about this time felt different.

I WAS DIRTY AND SMELLED LIKE SWEAT. I ALSO HAD A BAD CASE of helmet hair. The second Braeden was escorted off the field, I moved to go with him, but Coach reminded me there was a game to finish.

"You think I care about the game right now?" I'd growled through my helmet as I towered over him in my uniform.

"Walker is fine."

My stony silence made it clear what I thought about that shitty response.

Coach shook his head. "What I mean is he's conscious. His injuries are not life-threatening. You know this, Anderson. You just talked to him. We have five minutes left on the clock. Go finish this. Don't let them win because you're distracted."

The mouthguard between my teeth made an unpleasant sound with the way my teeth ground against it as I swung around to stare across the field at the other team. I was good at staying cool under pressure. I kept my head in the game, didn't take it personal.

Right now, though, it felt pretty fucking personal.

My eyes swept the sideline for the douche that had plowed into my brother. I knew this was a violent sport. I knew injuries happened, tempers ran hot, and egos crowded the turf. Most injuries were just hazards of the game, men playing balls to the wall.

The second my eyes locked onto the player who'd taken B down and caused a pileup, all reasoning became a magical myth I would have argued didn't even exist.

He was smirking. The very air around him was proud he'd taken down the Hulk. He saw me staring and lifted his chin in acknowledgment.

Fuck this guy.

"Holmes!" I roared around the purple guard shoved between my lips.

My running back appeared, slapping his hand on my shoulder. "Here, boss."

Coach made a rude sound.

We ignored him.

I leaned in. "I don't care what it takes. Get open and go long. We're going to the endzone and finishing this game."

Holmes slammed his hands together and nodded. "You got it."

"That's not the play I called," Coach barked.

"You told me to finish this game. I'm going to finish it."

The team took the field. The ball snapped into my palms. With single-minded focus, I trained all the frustration and pure fuck-you energy into my arm and fired the ball down the field to Holmes who broke free and went long.

All sound fell away. It was just me and the ball as it blazed right into the running back's arms. Snatching it out of the air, he turned and plowed into the endzone, and as he spiked the ball in victory, the noise of the stadium came back full force.

Game over.

Knights were going wild on the field as I locked eyes once more with the douche. He didn't look so smug anymore. With adrenaline pumping through my veins, I pointed right at him and started walking backward.

That one was for you.

He ripped his helmet off and scowled.

I flipped him off. Yeah, I was probably gonna get fined for that.

Worth the cash.

"Anderson!" Coach bellowed.

I jogged the rest of the way off the field. Special teams was lining up for the extra point. I wasn't sticking around for that. I did my job.

"Where the hell are you going?" Coach called after me.

"I'm done," I said and jogged off the field.

In the locker room, I followed the sound of voices to where Braeden and the medical team were assessing the situation. Most of them were standing outside the door, and I frowned but kept right on going. "He's on the phone," someone cautioned.

I shouldered through the door, taking in my brother in full gear, sans helmet, with his cell pressed to his ear. One of the physicians was stabilizing his knee, which was already three times its normal size and an ugly shade of purple. Seeing it was like a punch in my gut.

This is bad.

"You really don't need to come," B was saying into the line. He grunted. "Don't cry, Blondie. I'm fine."

"What's it looking like?" I asked Tom.

"We're taking him for imaging."

"Tear?" I asked.

Tom hesitated, then nodded. "Likely."

More like a guarantee, and we all knew it.

"I love you too," Braeden said. A moment later, he dropped the phone in his lap and looked at me. Lines were drawn around his mouth and eyes. Pain was riding him hard.

"Kids were crying. Girls are already packing."

I cursed beneath my breath and nodded. There was no point in arguing with them. They would come no matter what we said.

"Ambulance is ready to go," one of the men outside the door called.

"Let me take off these pads," Braeden grumped, reaching for his jersey.

I went forward and helped him, basically undressing him from the waist up. "Why aren't you on the field?"

"I finished the game," I said, clipped, tossing away all this shit. At his feet, Tom was pulling off his cleats and socks.

His pants were ruined because of the way they'd cut them to get to his knee.

"I'll get you some clothes," I said, starting for the door.

"Rome."

I stopped, turning back. A look passed between us. It said everything and nothing.

"Thanks," was all he said, his voice gruff.

I nodded once and went to get our clothes. I didn't bother to shower or wait for the rest of the team on the field. I threw on some sweats and got in the back of the ambulance with B.

And now here I was sitting in an empty room, unkempt and fucking worried while Braeden was down at imaging.

I wasn't worried about the results. I already knew what they were. It was a matter of severity. A matter of what was next.

The girls were still enroute, and I was glad it would take a little time to get here. It would let us get all the answers and give me some time with my brother.

The door to the room swung in, and a wheelchair appeared with B filling the seat. His busted leg was positioned straight out in front of him, a brace already in place.

His hair was in the same state as mine, and there were grass stains on his forearms. He looked tired, and his shoulders were slumped.

"How'd it go?" I asked, standing from the chair in the corner.

He glanced up instantly. "Considering no one bought me dinner before all those nudes they took, I'm gonna say not well."

The nurse pushing him rolled her eyes. "An MRI and an X-ray do not count as nudes."

"Peeping under my skin all the way to the bone seems pretty nosy to me."

"It's called medical care," she refuted, parking the chair beside the bed in the center of the room.

Braeden started to push up, and she made a sound. "Wait. Let me help you."

"I got it," I said, moving close to slip my arm around B and haul him up.

His body was stiff, but his muscles trembled either from exhaustion or pain, maybe both. The wheelchair slid back, and he reached for the bed, but I lifted him off his feet and up into a bridal-style hold.

His busted leg stuck straight out, and the gown he was wearing fluttered around him. "Hope you're wearing drawers. Otherwise, you really will be serving nudes."

"*Oh, Romeo,* what big muscles you have," Braeden said in a falsetto while fluttering his lashes.

"Not as big as your mouth."

"Think this is how Drew feels when Trent hauls him around?"

I laughed.

"We're going to keep your leg elevated with this," the nurse said, going around to the opposite side of the bed to grab a large foam wedge.

We got Braeden situated with his leg raised.

"I'll get some ice. Do you need anything else?" the nurse asked.

"Pain meds," Braeden's voice was gruff.

I glanced at his leg and frowned.

"I'm not sure it's time for those, but I'll check," she said.

The second the nurse was gone, Braeden released a breath and dropped his head against the propped-up mattress. "It's bad, Rome."

I knew he didn't mean the pain. He meant the injury.

Saying nothing, I grabbed the chair in the corner and dragged it right up to the side of the bed. I sat down, leaning forward to brace my elbows on the edge of the mattress. "We don't know anything yet. The results—"

"I heard it pop. I can't bear any weight on it at all. My knee is on fucking fire, but below it…"

My head whipped up. "Below it?"

"It's numb," he whispered.

I stood from the bedside and started to pace. Yeah, injuries were pretty much mandatory in football. But this sucked. "I should have fucking ground him into the turf."

Braeden made a gruff sound. "You know it's the game."

I snorted. It was a Rimmel-level snort. "Yeah? You didn't see the bastard's face after you left the field. I swear he got some twisted satisfaction in taking you out."

"The whole team was out for blood the entire game. You know that. They were hell-bent on getting revenge from the last time we handed them their asses."

I paced more. "Yeah? Well, they lost again."

"It wasn't personal, Romeo."

I stopped and turned to him.

"He saw his chance to tackle me, and he took it. I don't think he wanted to do this," Braeden said, gesturing to his leg.

The nurse came back, a large cold pack in her hand. She gingerly positioned it on his knee and stepped back. "The doc is on his way up with your results," she said. "He can also talk to you about pain management."

"Thank you," Braeden said.

The nurse glanced at me, then quickly away and hurried to the door.

It was barely latched when B cackled. "Never thought I'd see this day."

I raised an eyebrow.

"Me the calm collected one while you rage out."

"I'm not raging out," I bitched.

"You scared the nurse."

I gave him the finger.

There was a sharp rap on the door, and then it pushed open. A man in green scrubs and a lab coat walked in along with two of the team doctors and another doctor dressed the same as the first. The first doc had a tablet in his hand, and his buddy had a large envelope.

"Mr. Walker," the man with the tablet said. "I'm Dr. Granger. I'm the orthopedist on call tonight." He introduced himself. "And this"—he gestured to the man with the envelope—"is our resident sports medicine physician, Dr. Finnegan. And of course, you are familiar with your team physicians," he said, nodding at the men. "I'm assuming you gave consent for them to be here."

"Of course," Braeden said.

The team docs would be the ones coordinating his treatment and recovery.

Dr. Granger looked at me.

"Romeo Anderson," I said, gruff, but didn't offer my hand.

"He's my brother," B supplied.

"We have your results here." The doctor went on. "We've consulted—"

"Just tell me," Braeden said, impatience ripe in his tone.

"Unfortunately, it's a grade-three ACL tear."

Fuck.

"The meniscus is also torn."

I started pacing again.

Braeden said nothing, so the doctor continued.

"A grade-three tear occurs when the ACL is completely severed. That would explain why you can't bear any weight and the swelling and bruising are so severe."

A somber, morose mood dropped over the room. It made my skin feel tight, and I hated it.

"Because of the severity, you will need reconstructive surgery. We recommend waiting for about three weeks for the swelling to subside. We can also get you into some physical therapy leading up to it to try and regain some knee flexion. You will need to be in a brace at all times."

"And after?" I asked, jumping in before B.

"Recovery. Rehabilitation. Physical therapy."

"How long until I can play?" Braeden asked.

Tom spoke up. "You're out the rest of the season, Walker."

Dr. Granger cleared his throat. "Probably next season too."

Our eyes crashed. We shared a silent moment of pain, mourning, and *what the fuck*. Nine out of the ten years I'd been playing pro ball, B had been on the field with me. Sure, we both missed games for injuries and shit, but the rest of this season and *all* of next?

"With your age"—Dr. Granger interrupted our bro moment—"and pending any complications, it could be longer."

I swung to the doc, anger burning in my eyes. *"His age?"* I snapped. "He's in his early thirties."

"And you know that means he's practically geriatric in ball," Tom refuted.

I felt myself stiffen and rotated to our team doc. How dare he back up that outsider? Braeden was a Knight. Family. "What did you just say?" I said quietly. Deadly.

Tom cleared his throat.

"Sorry about him, Tom. He's on edge," B mused.

I gave my brother an irritated look. *Why isn't he freaking out? Why am I?*

They showed us the slides and the X-ray film, going into more detail. When they were done, Dr. Finnegan turned to Braeden. "You are in excellent physical shape. And while you might be a little old on the field, you are still young in years. You also have an excellent medical team. I see no reason why there will be complications from surgery."

"Maybe you should be on the team," I quipped, sliding a pointed glance at Tom.

He avoided my stare.

"What about pain management?" B asked, shifting a little. I could tell the pain was starting to worsen by the paleness of his skin and the way he gingerly adjusted the ice.

"Grade-three tears are painful. I can prescribe some stronger painkillers in lieu of over-the-counter anti-inflammatories."

"No." B was gruff. "Don't want anything too heavy. Wouldn't say no to some beefy ibuprofen, though."

Dr. Granger nodded. "We can get you a script for a higher dose because of your size and also so you don't have to swallow so many pills at the same time."

"Thanks."

"I'll note it in your chart and have the nurse bring some in," Dr. Granger said, doing something on the tablet in his hands. "Any other questions?"

"When's my surgery?"

"As I mentioned, it's best to do it in roughly three weeks. We can go ahead and get it scheduled before you leave."

I pulled my phone out of my pocket and hit the screen. "I'm calling Gamble."

"There's no need to call Ron Gamble," Tom said, his tone nervous.

I hit him with a pointed look. "You don't think there's a need to get the owner of this team and the most powerful man in the state on the phone so he can call in the best surgeon in the country?"

Dr. Granger bristled. "I'm perfectly capable—"

"This is my brother. I don't want capable. I want the best," I snapped and then turned my back to the room and pressed the phone to my ear.

Gamble picked up immediately. "Anderson. How is Walker?"

"He needs surgery. Complete ACL reconstruction."

"I'll make some calls," he said without me having to explain anything else.

"Three weeks from today." I informed him.

"I understand. I'll be in touch."

The call disconnected, and I shoved the device into my sweats. When I turned back, the room was empty and Braeden was in the center of the bed with a damn near gleeful look on his pasty face.

"What?" I grumbled.

"I'll never quit you, Rome!" he declared.

"Can you believe that guy? *Capable*," I muttered. I was gonna have to talk to Gamble about Tom. What a shitshow.

"He didn't seem like a bad dude."

"Did you hit your head?" I asked, going over to the side of the bed. "Did they check you for a concussion?"

B's laugh was more of a rumble in his chest. "You know I don't have a concussion."

"Then why are you being like this?"

"You mean like you?"

"That is not how I am," I said, jabbing a finger at him.

He snorted. We hung out with my wife way too much. "You mean calm and reasonable? Bet."

I scowled.

Reaching down, he fiddled with the cold pack again. His voice was quiet. "What the fuck else am I supposed to do? Ivy and the kids were crying. Rim was worried. You're being me. Someone has to be the calm one. Besides, I can't do pissed off and pain at the same time."

I felt my shoulders droop. "*Fuck*," I cursed beneath my breath. He was right. I was the calm one. The one the family called the alpha. I wasn't the one that roared and threw attitude. I was the one who smiled and charmed. Who kept everything together.

Except, right now, things feel like they're splintering apart.

It doesn't matter. Get your shit together. Your family needs you.

"I'm sorry, man." I rubbed my hand over my face, dried sweat flaking away under my fingertips. "I'm being an ass. I didn't mean to make this harder on you."

Guilt ate at my insides like acid. He was the one in the hospital bed. He was the one out of the game. *So close to the Bowl too.* But what was the first thing he did?

Called the fam. Reassured everyone. Smiled through the blow he'd just been delivered.

"Are you kidding? This is some good shit. Front row seat to the alpha unhinged. I haven't seen you like this since Lo-Lo was born."

"That nurse made Rimmel cry," I said, anger boiling my blood once more.

Braeden cackled.

I exhaled.

"Your rage kinda makes me feel better to be honest."

Braeden's admission lifted my eyes. "Yeah?"

He half smiled. "Gets it all out, and I don't even have to be the one to do it."

"I'm proud of you."

He blinked, a surprised light shining in his eyes before he blinked again, washing it away. Pressing a hand to his chest, he said, "That's the nicest thing you've ever said to me."

"Fuck off," I muttered, and then we both laughed.

When the humor died away, I sat on the edge of the mattress by his feet, making sure to not jostle his elevated leg. "Seriously, though. Braeden ten years ago would have been hulking out over this. Hell, Braeden five years ago probably would be too."

"You heard the docs. I'm geriatric now. Can't be acting a fool."

"You're not geriatric," I demanded, a hard edge lacing my tone.

"You having a midlife crisis?" he asked. "Freaking out about our age? Pretty sure we're both too young for that. But yeah, you wanna go buy some fancy sports car or a yacht to get it all out, I'm down. Hell, I'll pay half."

"A boat might be nice," I mused.

"We can't let Drew drive. We'd all end up puking over the side."

I laughed. His accident several years ago didn't keep him sidelined long. He was still a certified adrenaline #junkie.

Braeden hitched his chin. "What's up?"

"Nothing," I answered, decisive. "It just pissed me off when they told me to finish the game. When they came in here like they were telling you the weather and not about something that affects your whole life."

"I'm a big boy. I can handle it. Honestly, we're lucky we've played this long without any major injuries."

I stood. "We hanging out 'til the girls get here?"

B nodded. "I'll ice the leg a little longer, let these pain meds kick in. When the girls get here, they can grill the doc, and then he'll discharge us."

I glanced at the door. "I'll see if the doc will clear you to fly home tomorrow."

"You think you could maybe find some coffee too? Might help with the adrenaline crash."

My eyes went back to his face, searching. "How are you really?"

"In need of coffee."

"I'll be back in a few." I headed for the door. There was more for us to say, but I recognized we both needed a minute to process.

Downstairs, I found a coffee cart that was still open and ordered two lattes with double shots of espresso. I also grabbed some bottled water and two donuts with pink frosting and sprinkles out of the case.

I was sort of glad we were in New York because I didn't get as much attention here as I would have if we were in Maryland, and it was nice to have even a small amount of anonymity.

'Course, maybe it was my black mood and un-showered ass that kept people away. Either way, I'd take it.

B's words echoed in my head, bothering me in a way I wish they didn't. Was I having some sort of midlife crisis?

I shook my head. That was Braeden talk. I was not having

a crisis. Still, I couldn't deny I felt unsettled. I had since my talk with Blue and then Rimmel. It felt like I was at a fork in the road. As if I could sense a shift in life... in our family. I'd been mulling over it for a couple weeks now.

It was distracting. And now my brother was in the hospital. I felt somewhat responsible. Rationally, I knew it was bullshit. But irrationally? What if what I'd been feeling had somehow affected B's game? Our game? What I'd somehow caused the shift I'd been worrying about?

Alphas were supposed to be the strongest. Impenetrable. What if this was a sign?

Outside of B's room, I heard the rumble of his voice, but it was low enough I couldn't make out what he was saying. I didn't bother hesitating. We invaded each other's personal space more often than we respected it, so why would now be any different?

I strolled in, and he gestured with an old-school "what-up" nod. I held out his coffee, and he took it, instantly taking a sip.

"You're my hero," he mouthed. "That's all I know for now, Mom."

He made a few noises as he drank more coffee. "Yeah, icing it now... Yeah... Will do... Okay." He glanced at me. "Mom says hi."

"Hi, Mom," I called as I lowered into the chair beside his bed.

"She said she loves me more than you."

I heard her scolding him on the line, and I laughed.

"Kiss the kids for me," he told her.

When the call ended, he grabbed the bag I'd set beside him and shoved his face inside. "Sprinkles!" He groaned.

Diving one hand inside, he pulled out the pastry and shoved half in his mouth. *"Ohmygoddd,"* he practically prayed, shoving a quarter of what was left between his lips. "The one good thing about retirement is I can eat what I want when I want," he mused, shoving in the rest of the donut and chomping like a cow.

I froze. "What did you just say?"

He stopped chewing, his cheek still puffed out with food. "Rome—"

I stood up rapidly, the chair sliding across the floor behind me. "Who said anything about retirement?"

Heavy silence filled the room. It was so intense it was as if everything else faded away. All I knew was the heartbeat in my ears, the heat of the coffee in my palm, and the weight suddenly parked on my chest.

His quiet voice restarted the room but also left me reeling. "We both know there's no coming back from this."

"The fuck you just say?" I whispered, my eyes lasering into his face.

His dark head leaned against the mattress and rolled toward me. He dropped whatever shield he had in his eyes and let me see the pain and panic he was feeling. "I need my best friend right now, Rome. The one I can say anything to. The one who doesn't bullshit. I need that right now because, in about an hour, the fam will be here and…"

He didn't finish, but he didn't have to. I knew. Long ago, before Rimmel and Ivy—hell, even before Trent and Drew— it was just me and B. We had each other's backs from an early age, and while we still did, we'd shifted from brothers into family. The urge to protect him was screaming, but he didn't need my protection. He needed his brother.

I grabbed the chair and dragged it back to sit down. The coffee in my hand was abandoned to the bedside table, and I leaned in. "Lay it on me."

He took another sip of the coffee, and I waited, not rushing him. "This is a career-ender. We all know it."

"They didn't say—"

Amusement lit his eyes. "Because you practically ripped off their balls for calling me old."

"You aren't."

"We both know, in terms of football, I am. The average pro player's career lasts two and a half years, bro."

"We aren't average."

"Holler," he called, holding out his fist.

I bumped mine against it.

"Nine years is a long run." He went on.

My stomach tightened, but he didn't want me to argue. I was trying not to. I wanted him to pour it out before everyone arrived and he felt he couldn't.

"I know I'll come through the surgery fine. The recovery too. But my knee won't be the same. I've taken a lot of hits over the years. I feel it. I know you do too. I keep playing because I love the game. Because I'm fucking grateful. Because I can't imagine not playing with you..."

My eyes got misty. The air quality in this room was terrible.

"You know, I never in a million years would have guessed this would be my life," he mused. "I always knew you were destined for the NFL. That you'd be a hall-of-famer by the time you were thirty." Smiling, he shook his head. "I never thought I'd be one too."

"You deserve it. You're a damn good player," I said fiercely.

"Yeah. I am," he replied boldly. "And that's not something I would have ever been able to admit back in the day."

"Now you sound geriatric. *Back in the day*," I cracked.

"I want my cane to have a gold football on the top," he contemplated. "Engrave my name on the wood."

I laughed.

"For real, though." He went on. "Back at Alpha U, I was a total mess. Having fun, buried under the baggage of my dad and the belief I was just like him. I didn't expect a big future. Hell, just having your friendship and keeping myself from ending up like him seemed like enough."

"You're too good for that."

"Yeah, you made me see that. You nudged me into the NFL, talked me up even when I didn't deserve it. You fought for it even when it looked like it wouldn't happen and I'd given up. You made me believe I was worthy."

There was a lump in my throat. It made it hard to talk. "It was always gonna happen. With or without me."

He shook his head. "Don't downplay it, Rome. I did the work to haul myself out of that headspace but only because you held out your hand and helped me. I put in the work on the field, but I wouldn't have been on that field if you hadn't believed in me."

I lifted my shirt and swiped my eyes. "I'll never quit you, B," I said into the fabric.

"Me either. We're for life. Football or no football."

I stared at him.

"An entire year or more off the field. I'll be in shape with PT, but it's not gonna keep me conditioned, and I'll be even older when I'm cleared to play."

"You know I'll work with you. Just like you did when I broke my arm."

"We were twenty then," he refuted. "And yeah, I know you will." He was quiet a moment before his brown eyes met mine. "I want to go out on top. I don't want to come back and play like a secondhand version of myself."

I swallowed the thousands of protests coating my tongue. I swallowed so many I probably wouldn't be hungry for a month.

"I hate this," I confessed.

"I'm right."

I nodded. "You're right."

He expelled a deep breath, and it was as though a major weight lifted off his shoulders. Relief smoothed his features, the lines of pain softening around his eyes.

He needed to hear that. He needed me to say it.

"I know this isn't exactly going out on top… I mean…" He waved a hand at his bum leg. "But I've had a good season. Good stats. My career has been fucking impressive."

"It has." I agreed because it was the truth. Braeden Walker was one of the best running backs in professional football history.

His best shit-eating grin graced his face. "And when you take us to the Bowl and get me another ring… Well, is there any better way to retire?"

Yeah. With me. I didn't say it out loud.

"You'll get another ring," I vowed. If this was what he wanted, I'd make it happen.

"I know."

"You don't have to decide right now." I cautioned. "Maybe think about it. Talk to Ivy."

"Truth? I've been thinking about it a while."

I sat back. "What? You never said anything."

"You didn't either."

Shock must have rippled over my face because he laughed. "I know you, Romeo. I know when you got thoughts. It's been harder this season, right? To be gone so much."

I propped my dirty sneakers on the edge of the bed. "Yeah."

Braeden drank some more coffee and fished the other donut out of the bag. I waited until he took a bite and said, "That was for me."

"You can't eat this. You gotta win the Super Bowl."

"Asshole."

"I'm just looking out for you, bro. It tastes good. I'll enjoy it for you."

"I feel the love," I cracked.

"Rome." His voice was knowing. Sincere.

My shoulders drooped. "How am I supposed to play without you?"

"I might not be on the field, but I'll still be with you."

"That was corny."

"It's true."

"I worry I'm putting my dream over my family."

"I get that. The older the kids get, the harder it is to be away. But they know you love them, and you spend all your spare time at home. Plus, it's good to show them hard work pays off."

I didn't say anything, warring with myself over everything in my head and heart.

"It's only a few more years." B supplied.

My eyes widened.

"You want fifteen, right?"

"How'd you know that?"

"It's the bromance." He said it with a total straight face. "It knows things."

I scoffed, but deep down, I believed him.

"You have five more years in you. Hell, even then, you won't be at the age to have a midlife crisis," Braeden heckled. "We can still buy a yacht, though. Tie sweaters around our shoulders and drink dry martinis while we stand on deck in loafers."

I made a face. "No."

"Oh, thank God. I mean, I'll do it for you, Rome. But it was hurting my heart a little."

I laughed.

"It's my turn to tell you I believe in you. That I know you can do this. I'll be at home, keeping an eye on things now. If I get even a small whiff of anything that I think you need to be there for, I'll come get you myself."

"It's not your job to take care of my family," I argued.

"Newsflash, asshole. It's not your family. It's *ours*."

"You're right."

"I know," he said, shoveling the rest of the donut in his mouth. Sprinkles fell onto the ugly hospital gown.

"I really meant it when I said I was proud of you. You're a good man, and I'm proud to call you my brother."

"Bring it in," he said, holding out his arms.

Laughing, I leaned over the side and hugged him.

"Glad we had this talk. Kinda blows I had to smash my knee for it to happen, but I do it for you."

"If you change your mind, you decide you want to play—"

"You'll be there. I know." He nodded. "Honestly, though, this feels good." He made a face. "Not this," he said, pointing to his leg. "But the decision. It feels right. Now that I know you're cool."

"You've been worrying about this because of me?" I said, guilt once more piercing me.

"I'm a big boy." He interrupted my thoughts. "This ain't on you. I'd be lying if I said I wasn't worried about bringing up retirement, though. I was gonna try and hit fifteen with you."

"But you would have been doing that for me, not you."

He shrugged a shoulder. I opened my mouth, but he held up a hand. "And before you go acting all crazy, I wasn't distracted on the field. I wasn't just going through the game for you. I love football. It was an unfortunate tackle that hit in just the right spot."

Maybe, but it was an opportunity. For him to follow his heart and be home with the fam.

"You should retire," I announced.

"Thanks for the permission."

"Tell me you didn't need it," I countered.

He pursed his lips. "It's just nice to have is all."

I smiled. The first real smile of the entire night. "I just want you to be happy. We might not be teammates much longer, but we will always be brothers."

Braeden settled back into the bed, a large smile curving the lower half of his face. "I'm gonna start planning a bomb-ass retirement party for you. I got five years... This is gonna be epic."

"We gotta have yours first."

Down the hall, I heard Ivy call for Braeden.

"Incoming," I said, moving to the door so I could put an end to their worrying.

"Romeo?"

I turned back. "Hm?"

"Maybe let's keep my retirement on the DL for a while. Just between us." He pointed to his lower half. "This is gonna be enough drama for a while."

"Anything for you, bro."

"Don't forget about the ring!" he called. I laughed. "And the cane!" His voice followed me out into the hall.

Down near the nurses' station, Rimmel, Ivy, Trent, and Drew stood. Drew saw me first and told the group.

Ivy started running.

Rimmel followed suit. She tripped halfway down the hall, and I rushed forward, but Trent scooped her up before she face-planted in the hall. He didn't even put her down, just handed her off to me.

Inside the room, Ivy was already fussing over Braeden, and Drew was giving him shit about having a bum knee.

Rimmel climbed up my body, wrapping her legs around my waist. Her nose wrinkled, and her glasses dipped lower on her scrunched nose. "You smell."

"Kiss me anyway."

She did.

"Braeden?" she asked when we parted.

"There are sprinkles all over this bed." Ivy's exasperated voice carried out into the hall.

Rimmel giggled.

"He's gonna be just fine," I told her.

"And what about you, Romeo?" she asked, knowingly gazing into my eyes. "How are you?"

I kissed her again. "I'm all good, baby. All good."

5 Years Later...

THE PLANE WENT WHEELS DOWN ON AN AIRSTRIP THAT frankly could have passed for a bowling alley.

This cannot be safe.

Romeo's warm voice filled my ear, followed instantly by the rush of tingles down the back of my neck caused by the brush of his lips. "Even after all these years, you still hate flying."

"Don't you make fun of me, Roman Anderson," I said even as I squeezed my eyes shut. The plane jostled and bounced on its wheels, and the grip I had on his hand intensified.

"I know I just retired, but I'd still like to retain the use of my hand," he mused.

Gasping and eyes flying open, I stared down at his fingers that were red from how hard I was squeezing them. "I'm sorry," I apologized, lifting his hand to kiss the backs of his fingers.

"I don't think that's good enough, smalls. You better kiss them again."

He was a lying liar, but I kissed his fingers again anyway. "This plane is practically a tin can," I whispered.

"Smells kinda like tuna."

I spun around to see Braeden's face—well, part of it—squished between the seats as he tried to join the conversation. He looked so stupid that I laughed out loud and lifted Romeo's hand to smash it against my lips and muffle the sound.

"Chicken of the sea," Braeden said again, his lips flapping between the narrow space.

Romeo laughed.

"Braeden, honestly," Ivy said, but she was laughing too.

His face disappeared back into his row. "Say it ain't so, Blondie. It's fishy as hell in here."

"Shhh," I scolded, worrying he might hurt the pilot's feelings.

"We're going to a tropical island. The fish smell is free," Ivy whispered.

"For what I paid, we should be getting caviar and champagne for free, not stank," he muttered.

This time, I leaned over and buried my face in Romeo's arm to muffle the laugh I could not hold in. I swear, my BBFL got even more ridiculous with age.

Romeo's shoulders shook with laughter, but he glanced over the seat into the row behind us. "I told you I—"

"I will toss you out of this plane, Anderson." Braeden cut him off. "You better get your man, sis. He's trying to ruin my present."

I patted Romeo's arm. "Now, Romeo. Let your brother spend obscene amounts of money on you."

He snorted.

"A guy tries to do something nice," B mumbled, and Ivy consoled him.

The plane put on the brakes, and my body was thrust forward. Romeo put his arm in front of my chest to hold me in the seat while the plane finally came to a stop. The second we were still, I pushed his arm and looked across the aisle to where Blue and Jax were sitting.

They seemed to not notice the rough landing and were already staring out the window in fascination. Leaning around a bit more, I looked to the row behind them where London and Asher sat side by side. Seeing me, Ash gave me a thumbs-up and a smile.

A few moments later, we were escorted off the plane and onto the tarmac where several white limousines waited. Farther down the runway, another plane just like ours touched down. I let out a breath I hadn't even realized I'd been holding the second it smoothed out and taxied forward.

"Safe and sound," Romeo rumbled in my ear.

I glanced up at him and smiled.

"What about the others?" I wondered. Our immediate family was here, but everyone else was still en route.

"Another plane will be here soon, and then the others are coming in a little later," Braeden said. "We should all be here by tonight."

"I had no idea you were so organized, Braeden. I'm impressed." I teased him. He'd been planning this "retirement party" for Romeo for years now. It practically became his hobby while recovering from his complete ACL tear. Almost the entire time he planned, he refused to tell any of us anything about it and was sneaky and secretive. When he finally revealed the big surprise, I was, well, surprised. It was way fancier and more involved than I expected.

Braeden sauntered over, slinging his arm around my

shoulders. "Let your big brother teach you the way," he said. "I am the king of gift-giving. This here is the best gift Rome's ever got."

"What about the four kids I gave him?" I always counted Evie even if she was in heaven with her grandmother.

Braeden scoffed. "He had to work for those too. Plus, he pays for them. This is all free," he said, spreading his arm to gesture to everything.

"Yes, that ride in the tuna can was super fun. Thanks," I deadpanned.

He glanced at me and winked. "Just wait 'til you see what you have to ride in next."

I blanched. "I hope you mean that limo over there."

"After that."

My stomach sank. "Braeden…"

As if he could sense my nerves, Romeo appeared, pulling me away from Braeden and into his arms. "What's the matter, baby?"

"Now, sis, you know I'd never bring you somewhere unsafe," B said, trying to calm me down, but the damage was already done.

Romeo was frowning when I glanced up. "I thought we were here."

His brows drew down. "We are," he said, glancing at B for confirmation. "Right?"

"About that…" Braeden hedged.

"Braeden," Ivy warned, popping a hand on her hip. Her high blond ponytail was a little rumpled from all the traveling we'd done today. Which, frankly, was so much.

The only reason I'd agreed to all of this was for Romeo. For our entire family.

Even if I clearly didn't know what this was.

"Mom! Are those limos for us?" Nova called, the wind

blowing her long brown hair across her face. At fifteen, she was as tall as me now. She was also so beautiful with her long, shiny brown hair, blue eyes, and wide, high cheekbones.

"Ask your father," Ivy said, and we all turned to look at Braeden.

"I feel attacked."

"Dad?" Nova questioned.

"Of course it's for you, Critter." *Yep.* He still called her that. Poor girl. "Can't be having my girls ride in anything less than they deserve."

"Uncle Romeo!" A voice blew in with the wind. "We're here!"

Our attention turned to the rest of the family heading over from the second plane. Andi waved enthusiastically from Trent's back with Drew and Travis at their side. Romeo's parents, Anthony and Valerie, were right behind them along with Braeden's mom and stepfather, Caroline and John.

She patted her dad's shoulder, and Trent bent down so she could hop off and run at Romeo.

He caught her and lifted her into his arms. "How was the plane ride, Peanut?"

"Bouncy," she said. "I think Grandma Valerie is sick."

"Moms, you need a barf bag?" Braeden called, going to Valerie's side.

She did look a little green.

"I raised you better than that," Caroline admonished him.

"Pardon," Braeden corrected. "How are you feeling, moms?"

Valerie gave him a wilted smile. "Please just tell me we're here."

Once again, all eyes turned to Braeden.

"So, ah, we have one more ride after this," he said, sheepish.

"What kind of ride?" I asked warily.

He blanched. "Well, it's an island resort," he hedged.

Drew laughed. "Should have warned some people."

"I was trying to keep as much a surprise as I could," he reasoned.

"Braeden James, tell us everything right now," Ivy demanded.

"I rented out an entire private island resort."

"An entire resort?" Romeo seemed speechless.

"My brother only retires from an epic fifteen-year career as a pro football player once in his life," B told him. "You had to dig deep these last couple years to get there. I couldn't just bake a cake."

"What's wrong with baking a cake?" I asked. That's exactly what I'd done when he came home. I had balloons and streamers too.

He blanched. "Nothing, sis. We like your cake. This is brother stuff."

I rolled my eyes, and Romeo wrapped his arms around me from behind. "I loved your streamers and cake, baby."

"Well, it's no private island," I muttered. Who even thinks to rent out an entire resort?

Of course, Romeo sponsored and paid for an entire parade in the Knights's hometown for Braeden when he retired. Built him a giant float with a throne on it that B sat in the entire time. It was ridiculous and made national news.

Must be that brother stuff Braeden was going on about.

"Do the Maldives even have resorts that can be exclusively rented?" Valerie asked, looking less peaked.

When B said a vacation to the Maldives, we were all picturing fruity cocktails and beach chairs… not insane flight time and a private island.

Braeden spread his arms. "We're here, aren't we?"

"Get to the seaplanes," Drew said, glee in his eyes.

I gulped. "Seaplanes?"

"Like I said, our resort is its own exclusive island. There are twenty-six houses, some over-the-water bungalows and some right on the beach. There's a full staff, clubhouse, and a swim-up bar. Actually, there's a lot of pools. We have all access to snorkeling and non-motorized water equipment."

Drew made a disappointed sound.

"Slow your roll, Mask," Braeden told him. "We have some designated times for wave runners and speed boats."

Drew and Travis high-fived. Speed demons, the both of them.

"We have the entire island to ourselves?" Ivy asked.

Braeden nodded. "Yep. No paparazzi and a staff that signed NDAs. We need the room anyway. There's thirty-six of us total."

Romeo made a shocked sound. "Thirty-six?"

Braeden nodded. "Arrow, Hopper, Joey and Lorhaven, and their kids aren't the only ones coming." He grinned. "Liam Mattison and his entire fam is en route too."

My jaw dropped. "Bellamy and Sabrina are coming too?"

"Yep. Daniel, Meredith, and their daughter too."

"We get to see everyone!" I exclaimed.

He beamed. "An entire week with our entire family in a tropical paradise."

Ivy threw her arms around Braeden. "This is incredible! Worth every penny!"

He hugged her tight and grinned over her shoulder. "Makes the seaplane ride worth it, right?"

"What's a seaplane?" Andi asked.

"A plane that takes off and lands in water," Trent explained. "Instead of the wheels like what's on those planes"

—he pointed to the ones we just exited—"a seaplane has pontoons on the bottom to make it float."

Andi pursed her lips. "So it's a flying boat?"

"My girl is a genius," Drew mused.

"Aren't seaplanes small?" Caroline asked.

"They seat five." Braeden confirmed.

Five? This made the tuna can look like a good time.

"How are we all gonna fit?" London asked.

"We have more than one, sweetheart. And we'll all just take turns until we're all on the island," Braeden explained.

"Cool! Can we go first?" Jax asked, gesturing between him and Blue and Asher.

I leaned into Romeo.

"Adults will be riding with all the kids," he declared.

"The limos are going to take us all to the lounge while immigration sorts our passports, and then we can leave five at a time on the seaplanes."

"I think I might need that barf bag after all," Valerie whispered to Anthony.

I nodded in agreement.

"C'mon, fam! This is for the end of an era and the beginning of a new one!" Braeden declared.

"We're down," Drew said, and Trent nodded.

"My brothers." Braeden approved.

"Of course, son. This is a once-in-a-lifetime trip." Anthony agreed.

"You went all out, B. I'll never quit you," Romeo said, stepping away from me to hug him.

When they were done, Braeden looked between Ivy and me.

"Of course we're in," I said. "We've already been traveling for twenty hours. What's a few minutes more in a seaplane?"

"How long is the ride, Braeden?" Ivy asked.

"Less than twenty minutes."

The kids started bouncing all over the place, all with more energy than I would ever possess again, and we were directed to the limos where we were escorted to a very nice lounge with air-conditioning and glasses of champagne.

I drained mine and reached for another. I was getting on a seaplane.

8

FUCKING FIFTEEN.

I made it. Seemed a little surreal that I was officially retired. Especially when about five years ago, I had so many doubts. Worrying I was hurting my family by not being home more. Putting unnecessary pressure on my kids by being "famous." Doubting I could make it to fifteen when B was injured and decided to retire.

In the end, I rallied.

We all did.

Braeden had his surgery and went through recovery and PT. Only then did he publicly announce he was retiring, which was a blow to the Knights and fans everywhere. He stuck to his guns, though, and remained firm it was what he wanted. I admired him for that. For who he'd become.

He was a good father and husband. A damn good ball player. My best friend.

And now? He was a damn good coach. Imagine that.

Hothead Braeden the head coach of our old high school football team, the Green Hornets. He would always be "The Hulk," but he was a lot less hotheaded now, and it was epic to watch him come into his own and settle into the life he was meant to have.

In a way, it inspired me to go for my dream of fifteen. Whenever I doubted it, they were there. My #fam.

With the kids older, it was easier for Rimmel to travel with them. They came to more games, and I felt like I was missing a little less time. They were my unofficial but most important cheer squad, and I realized Rimmel was right. I never had to choose. I was a lucky bastard who had it all.

It was bittersweet to be here fifteen years later, an entire career to look back on and a future spread out with possibilities. I set records, had hands filled with rings, and was arguably the most famous quarterback in pro football. It was a legacy I was proud to leave behind.

The sky was still bright, the sun lowering in the sky as the day inched toward night. The water was crystal-clear, the purest turquoise I'd ever seen. The sand was white and the balmy breeze unlike anywhere else I'd ever been. The fronds on the many mature palm trees rubbed together, creating their own island music, perfectly complimenting the sounds of the ocean waves.

The deck was warm underfoot as I stepped out of the bungalow, heading straight for my wife who stood staring out over the endless water and sky view. Her hair was down and knotted in every direction from the wind. The loose yellow dress she wore fluttered around her small frame.

Even in her thirties, after four kids, she looked like the same girl I'd met all those years ago at Alpha U.

The soft material of the billowing dress plastered against my legs when I wrapped around her from behind and buried my face in the side of her neck. Tilting her head, she hummed while wrapping her arms over mine at her middle.

"This view is incredible," she said, scratching her fingers into my overly long blond hair.

I pressed a kiss against the soft skin of her throat and lifted my face to admire the view she was so smitten with. "We need to go over the ground rules."

She stiffened. "Ground rules."

"We're staying in a bungalow with miles and miles of water around us. Did you think there wouldn't be rules?"

She gasped with indignation and spun in my arms to glare. Even after all these years, she was adorable as hell.

"I am not one of your children, Roman Anderson," she sassed. "I do not need rules."

"You fell at the animal shelter last month and sprained your wrist."

"The floor was wet."

"Yeah, a little spill on the floor," I mused, turning her to look at the ocean. "Look at all this ocean."

"*Obviously*, I didn't see the spill. But obviously, *all this ocean* is hard to miss," she retorted.

Over her shoulder, I smiled. "Need I remind you of the time you got lost in the woods in Colorado and almost got eaten by wolves?"

She groaned, tossing her hands up for extra dramatics. "You just won't forget about that, will you?"

I nipped at her shoulder. "No."

"There are no wolves here."

"There's sharks." Not to mention, up until we had kids, she refused all contact with water, and now here we were, sleeping in an over-the-water bungalow. She did know how to swim—we made sure of it—but it would never be her strong suit.

Her snort got carried away on the wind. "I'd like to enjoy my vacation."

"Me too. Which is why there are rules."

"Okay, Roman." She turned to face me, looping her arms around my neck. "Let's hear these rules."

"Rule number one," I started, and she rolled her eyes.

I kissed her nose.

"No swimming without me."

She sniffed. "As if I even want to swim."

"No swimming without me," I repeated. "Rule number two," I said, letting go of her to reach down and pick up the bag near my feet. "You have to wear this at all times."

Making a face, she reached into the bag and pulled out a neon-yellow boyshort wetsuit with built-in floatation.

"What in the world is thing?" she wondered, staring at the fabric dubiously.

"Your new bathing suit."

She dropped her hands at her sides and scowled. "It has floaties built into it."

"It's for protection."

"It's so bright it can be seen from outer space!"

"That's the point." I confirmed. It was really hard not to laugh. But if I laughed, she'd be even more irate.

"This is ridiculous."

"Rule number three—"

"Three!"

"Don't go off on your own."

"It's a small island. Where would I go?" she asked.

"Knowing you, you'd somehow find a pack of Pygmies and get yourself kidnapped as their new mascot or some shit."

"That's the most ridicu—"

"Rule four." I interrupted.

Her nostrils flared. "I can't believe you even *allowed* me to come on this trip. How exhausting it must be to be married to a woman who can't function without rules. Maybe you should let the Pygmies have me!"

So much for holding it in. I laughed.

Her eyes narrowed.

Abort! Abort! "Now, baby…"

"Don't you *now baby* me, Roman Anderson. I've had enough," she said, spinning around behind me to give me a big shove in the center of my back.

I stumbled toward the edge of the deck but planted my weight to keep from toppling over. "Are you trying to drown me?"

"I think you need to cool off your swollen head."

I laughed again, and she took advantage of it to give me another shove.

I turned as I toppled and grabbed her hand, pulling her into the water with me.

She screamed, and water splashed as we plunged into the crystalline ocean. I blinked open my eyes, catching the way her dark hair floated around her head before pulling us to the surface. She sputtered and coughed even as she wound her legs around my waist.

"Romeo!" she sputtered, pushing her askew glasses up on the top of her soaked head.

I chuckled, treading water while she clung to me like a little octopus. "Rule four, keep your watch on at all times."

"Yes," she bemoaned, holding up her wrist. "This giant Apple Watch with a tracker inside so you can stalk my every movement."

I didn't bother pointing out it wasn't stalking if she was a whole hazard to herself. She'd probably try and drown me.

Wrapping one arm around her slim waist, I hugged her to me. The water was warm and brushed against us like a soft caress. "I can't help it, sweetheart. You're my whole world. I'm going to do everything I can to protect you."

Water dripped off the tip of her nose and clung to her lashes. "Oh, Romeo."

"Kiss me in the ocean, smalls."

Her lips were warm compared to the water drops clinging our skin, and our lips parted at the same time, tongues reaching out in tandem. She tasted like home and the sea as the golden rays of the sun sank lower in the sky.

"I'm not wearing that wet suit," she declared when we pulled apart.

"How about you wear it when we're all swimming?" I reasoned.

She pursed her lips. "Fine."

"I love you."

Her face softened. "I love you too."

I swam the short distance to a netlike hammock built into the edge of the deck and hoisted her inside, then hauled in behind her. The netting dipped with our combined weight, and we lowered closer to the water.

Rim's dress and hair were plastered against her. My T-shirt was soaked and sticking to my skin, so I pulled it off and tossed it onto the deck.

"If you had told me fifteen years ago that I would agree to sleep in a bungalow literally over the ocean, I would have laughed in your face," she mused, gazing out over the view.

"We can move to one of the beachfront cottages," I told her. Frankly, I would prefer it.

"The kids really wanted to stay in this one," she said. "I'll be okay if I can sleep in your arms."

"Where else would you be?"

She moved to crawl closer, her hand slipped through the net, and she tumbled into me.

I grunted. "And you wonder why we have rules," I muttered.

She giggled, and I pulled her into my lap.

"I can't believe Braeden did all this," she mused, snuggling closer.

"Being married to Ivy has rubbed off on him. Boy can plan an event."

Rimmel laughed.

"Romeo?"

"What, baby?"

She lifted her head from my chest, blinking up at me with slightly unfocused eyes. My heart somersaulted, and I smiled softly, tugging the glasses from her head to set them aside on the deck.

"You know I'm so proud of you, right?"

I palmed the back of her head. "I know."

"A cake, streamers, and balloons doesn't really compete with—"

"Hey." My voice was gruff when I cut her off. "There is no competition."

"I know," she said softly. "But I don't want you to think I'm not in awe of you."

My smile was fast. "You're in awe of me, huh?"

She rolled her eyes but then nodded. "Even after all this time, I still have to remind myself I'm not dreaming. That you are really real. I was always determined to make a life for myself," she confided. "But this? What we have, this is so much more."

"We're lucky," I confirmed, stroking her wet hair.

She shook her head. "It's not luck. It's you. We're all a family, and we all play our part, but you, Romeo, are the glue that holds this entire family together. You are the reason this life feels more like a dream. You've given us all so much. *Me* so much. I never in a million years would have believed love like this was possible if you hadn't fought for me."

"I'll always fight for us, baby. You and the kids."

"I know. And you did all of that while still living your dream. While becoming a football legacy." She went on. "I'm proud of you. The man you are, the way you played, and how much you accomplished. I know it was hard, and you sacrificed sleep and time and probably so much more I don't know about to be everything to everyone and still be a legend."

"This isn't going to help the big head you think I have," I teased. But even as I teased, a lump of emotion tightened my throat.

"You can have a big head just this once."

I laughed.

"My player," she murmured, cupping the sides of my face with her hands. "It's been a pleasure to watch you the last fifteen years. I can't wait to see what you do in the next fifteen."

"Maybe I'll just glue myself to your side and see how long it takes for you to get sick of me."

"Never," she swore.

"You just tried to down me."

She scowled. "That swimsuit is for a five-year-old."

"I had it made especially for you."

She rocked back, my hands cradling her waist. "You did?"

"Soon as Braeden said ocean, I had it ordered." I made a face. "Well, technically, Ivy ordered it, but I asked her to."

"She does have all our measurements," Rimmel recollected.

"I got one made for Lo-Lo and Andie too."

"You're so sweet."

I would have had one made for Nova, but at fifteen and as

fashionable as her mother was, I knew she'd never wear it. I'd just let B deal with all that.

"You're happy?" Rim asked, drawing my eyes off the horizon and back to her.

"How could I be anything less?"

"So you're sure you're ready to retire?"

I chuckled. "Everyone thinks I'm gonna go stir-crazy, don't they?"

"We love you. We're worried. *I'm* worried," she confessed.

"Why you worried, sweetheart?" I whispered, scooping her closer. She turned, winding her legs around my waist.

"I just don't want you to retire unless you are really ready. You know I'll support you playing as long as you can."

I kissed her as the breeze swirled around us and the waves knocked gently against the deck, letting my hands slide down her back against her saturated dress.

Feeling how wet it was, I began gathering it in my hands and tugging up to peel it off. Our lips popped, and she sat back, raising her arms. I tugged the fabric free and tossed it aside.

The second I saw what she had on beneath it, I laughed.

"You aren't the only one that can have swimsuits made." She arched her back to show me more of the design.

She was dressed in a navy-blue one piece with a gold #24 on the front. Smiling, she turned to show me the back, which had my name in gold.

Growling, I tugged her against me. "You know I love having my name on you."

"I know it's not purple like the Knights, but to me, our colors will always be from Alpha U."

"If we didn't have kids running around here somewhere, I'd peel this suit off you and fuck you right here."

"Later," she promised.

"This is perfect," I said, tracing my fingers over my name on her back. "Especially now."

She glanced over her shoulder. "Now?"

"Want to hear a secret?"

"Spill that tea, Anderson!" she exclaimed, scrambling around to face me once more.

I laughed. "Did the kids teach you that?"

She lifted one hand, palm up. "It's what everyone says."

"Before we left yesterday, I got a call."

"From whom?"

"My old coach at Alpha U."

Her eyes widened. "He wanted to congratulate you?"

I nodded. "He did." I smiled. "He also offered me a job."

Her eyebrows flew up. "A job?"

"Seems he's ready to retire. Said he was holding out as long as he could in hopes I'd be retiring too."

Her lips parted. Joy lit her face. "He wants you to coach the Wolves?"

I nodded.

Her squeal floated out over the water, and she tackled me. I sprawled back, the netting bouncing with our movements. "Oh my goodness, Romeo! That's so exciting."

"You think so?"

She scrambled up, practically elbowing me in the side. This girl was a one-woman show.

Straddling my waist, she laid her hands on my chest. "Oh, do you not want to take the job?" she said. Then, quickly, "If you don't want to, you shouldn't. I want you to be happy. I know that sports channel offered you that announcer-thingy position."

"That job is on the other side of the state," I pointed out. It was a lucrative-as-hell deal, though.

"We could make it work."

Reaching up, I caressed her cheek. "You would make it work, wouldn't you?"

"I'd do anything for you."

"I took the job at Alpha U."

Her body nearly vibrated with excitement. "Really?"

"How could I pass up the chance to go back to where it all started for us? For me?"

She shook her head emphatically. "Oh, no, Romeo. It started for you the day you were born. Football is in your DNA."

"Maybe so." I agreed. "But you're my heart. And I'm tired of being away from you. The kids. Now I can see you every single night."

Tears glimmered in her eyes, and the sun painted her skin golden. "I would love that."

"Me too." Then, "But I'll still have some away games."

She nodded. "It's okay."

"I love you."

A sob broke from her chest. "If I loved you any more, I swear my heart would explode."

"No exploding," I commanded, and she laughed.

"Maybe let's keep this between us a little longer. Let's just enjoy the vacation and my retirement before we tell everyone what's next."

"Whatever you want."

I raised an eyebrow. "Whatever?"

The sound of a seaplane in the distance interrupted my lusty thoughts. Her face lifted to the sky, but it wasn't in sight.

"Dad!" Blue hollered, a door in the bungalow slamming. "Liam's here!"

"This whole family is a damn cock block," I bemoaned.

Rimmel laughed, but before I could sit up, she stretched

out over me, her body rubbing against mine like a cat. "Later, remember?"

"Oh, baby, I won't forget."

9

RIMMEL

THE ENTIRE FAMILY WAS TOGETHER, AND THE BACKDROP OF THE unexpected reunion was more beautiful than any photo or painting I'd ever seen.

The sun had nearly set, the horizon on fire with hues of orange and yellow that gave way to a deep-purple sky that would eventually turn navy and light up with stars. The ocean glittered like a giant diamond under a spotlight, its ever-moving state an endless draw to the eye.

We were at the clubhouse on the island with its outdoor cabanas, flickering tiki torches, and lanterns glowing in the sand. A large table was laid out with enough food for a small country, but considering how many of us were here, it wouldn't go to waste. The fruit offering was drool-worthy, all of it fresh and oversized and artfully arranged beside many other dishes and breads that seemed too pretty to eat.

Off to the side was a pig roast, something I was actively trying not to look at. I was sure the taste was wonderful, and

I appreciated the work the staff here put into making such a feast, but I didn't think I could bring myself to enjoy that particular delicacy.

Two bartenders were on staff behind the large tiki bar, the sound of a whirring blender promising piña coladas aplenty.

Kids laughed and ran by in a blur.

"No running by the pool!" I called after them.

"I honestly had no idea a place this beautiful actually existed."

I smiled wide, spinning in the direction of the familiar voice. "Bellamy!" I exclaimed, rushing forward to hug her. We did greet them at the dock when they flew in but parted after so they could choose a bungalow and get settled.

"It's so good to see you," Bellamy said as we embraced.

When I pulled back, I stepped into a hug from Liam. "You guys look great. You haven't aged at all since we saw you last."

"I think the island lighting is playing tricks," Bellamy teased. There was no trick, though. Her thick, long blond hair was halfway down her back and wavy from the ocean breeze. Her skin was smooth and clear, and the only hint of age was the smile lines around her mouth. Even after four kids, she was trim, something I knew she worked at given that she was a chef and around food all day.

Shaking his head, Liam tugged his wife into his side. "No, Bells. You're just forever beautiful."

She smiled and poked him in his lean waist. "Maybe it's the cold weather at BearPaw," she teased. "It slows down our aging. Because you are still as handsome as you were when I met you at sixteen."

She was right. I didn't know what it was about the men in this family, but these guys were like fine wine and only got better with age. The scruff, lines around their eyes, and maturing features only made them more appealing.

He kissed her temple when she turned to me. "But trust me. Four kids are enough to age anyone."

"*And* two successful restaurants!" I put in.

After the couple completed their family with Shaw, Noah, Everly, and Wyatt, Bellamy finally realized her dream of opening a ski-up snack shack at BearPaw Resort. Well, she called it a snack shack. I called it a full-on restaurant. But she owned the place. It was an instant hit, so they opened another inside the resort with a similar vibe but bigger menu.

"I'm very lucky," she said.

"You work hard." Liam corrected her.

"We all do," I declared. "Which is why it's so great we could all get away. Braeden really outdid himself with this trip."

Romeo appeared soundlessly behind me. For such a large man, he was very graceful. After planting a kiss on top of my head, he hugged Bellamy and shook hands with Liam.

"B's gonna be insufferable after this."

"Poor Ivy." Bellamy agreed, and we all laughed.

"How's things at BearPaw?" Romeo asked Liam.

"Running smooth," he replied.

"Of course they are. I'm in charge," Alex cracked, approaching hand in hand with Sabrina. He held out his hand to Romeo. "The man of the hour." His teeth flashed. "Congratulations on fifteen years of greatness. You did the work. We get the vacay."

"Don't be an ass," Braeden joked, sneaking up behind me and lifting me off my feet.

I gasped, and he laughed, plunking me back down on the deck.

"So easy," he mused.

Another round of greetings went around, and then Braeden and Alex settled into their usual routine of firing insults at each other.

In their thirties and they still acted like children.

"At it again, I see," Ivy mused, approaching with two pineapples in hand, both of them with a straw and little umbrellas sticking out of the top.

"They're going to be like this when they're eighty." Sabrina agreed.

Her dark hair was pulled up in a twist, and she had a white tropical flower behind one of her ears.

Ivy handed me one of the piña coladas. I reached for it, but Romeo plucked it out of her hands and took a pull from the straw.

"Get your own," I told him.

After swallowing, he offered it to me. "Virgin. Good job, princess."

"If I had known it would meet your approval, I'd have added extra rum," Ivy told him, and he laughed. Her blue eyes found mine, face sheepish. "I just figured after all the travel and with all the water around…"

I smiled. "Definitely a good call. I'd be passed out in a palm tree after two sips."

"Now see here. There will be no drama on this trip." Braeden told the group. "Nothing but good times allowed."

"About that," Liam put in, a twinkle in his gray eyes as he held up a white bag I hadn't noticed before. "We brought you something, Rimmel."

I took the offered gift, reached inside, and groaned. "Not you too!" I exclaimed, pulling out a neon-orange life jacket.

Romeo laughed.

"Maybe you should put that on now," Alex suggested.

I scowled at his handsome face and twinkling icy-blue eyes. "I don't need a life jacket to eat dinner."

"Knowing you, you'd find a way to fall in the ocean with your plate," Daniel said as he and his wife, Meredith, joined the group. "Probably find a dolphin and tame it."

Meredith smacked him in the middle, but he laughed.

After pushing the ridiculous life jacket into Romeo's hands, I hugged them both. "Where is Selene?" I asked, looking around for their only daughter.

"She and Everly went to find Nova," Meredith replied, tugging her long dark braid over her shoulder.

"They're on the beach," Daniel said more precisely and muttered off a string of coordinates, which was probably the exact location of his daughter.

"I see you haven't changed," I mused, taking in his dark hair that was peppered with gray.

"That's my daughter," was all he said.

Ivy laughed, and Meredith winked.

All the men were overprotective around here, but Daniel… I think he probably took the cake.

"How is the veterinary clinic?" I asked Meredith.

She smiled. "Busy as ever. I was finally able to hire on another full-time vet, so I'm hoping to have more time off."

"Well, you're off to a good start," Ivy told her, gesturing to the gorgeous view.

"I agree. This place is stunning. A far cry from the mountains of Colorado."

"All right, guys," Braeden said, "the bar awaits." He flung his arms toward the cabana and waiting bartenders.

Everyone started to move in the direction of the drinks, but Braeden planted himself in the Ivy's and my path. "Not you two. You're cut off."

"Excuse me?" Ivy asked.

Braeden's eyes narrowed on the giant pineapple in her hand. "What the hell is that?"

"Something you're about to wear," Ivy intoned, sweet as pie.

"Blondie, if you want me to take my shirt off, you just need to ask."

"They're virgin," Romeo told him.

Braeden grunted. "Good looking out, Rome."

Ivy and I shared a look, then turned back to Braeden.

"Life jackets," I said.

"Restricted drinking," she said.

"Rules."

She made a sound. "It's like they think they're the boss of us."

Braeden's brown eyes were wide. "Now wait just a minute."

We stepped toward him. He stepped back.

I set my drink on a nearby table, and Ivy did the same.

"Now, I'm just trying to—"

We grabbed him by the arms and yanked him toward the pool. We got maybe three steps before he planted his big feet and refused to budge.

"Braeden James Walker, you let us punish you!" I hollered.

"You deserve it, bonehead!"

"I can't do it. I'm about to get my eat on." Braeden refused.

Ivy and I shared another look.

Braeden made a sound.

"Jax!"

"Blue!"

We both yelled at the same time.

"Oh, hells no!" Braeden roared.

A whole pack of kids appeared, and Braeden stood no chance. He went over the side of the pool with a massive splash.

Right after, the kids all leaped in after him, waves splattering the concrete and my feet.

With a roar, Braeden hoisted himself out of the pool, water plastering his board shorts and Hawaiian shirt to his muscular body. Dark hair lay heavy against his forehead and water dripped off his scowling brows. His attention zeroed in on his wife, and she shrieked and turned to run.

He caught the hem of her sundress when it billowed out around her hips as she spun. In seconds, he had her swung up into his arms, heading back to the pool.

"I just did my makeup!" she hollered. "Drew!"

"He can't help you now."

"Do not throw me in that pool, Braeden James. We are about to—"

Splash!

When she came up sputtering, Drew reached over the edge to offer his hand. But instead of having him help her out, she pulled him in.

"What the hell, Ives?" he complained, wiping the water from his face.

"That's what you get!" she told him.

From the side, Trent laughed.

"Keep laughing, frat boy," Drew called. "You're next."

Travis appeared, wrapping his arms around Trent in a bear bug and bulldozing him over the edge. Even though Trent was much bigger than his son, he was surprised, and his large body made a giant splash when he hit the water.

After that, all hell broke loose and an epic water battle broke out.

Romeo lifted me off my feet, and I went rigid, but he whispered in my ear, "That's no place for you."

He carried me away from the chaos and to a table where Joey, Lorhaven, Hopper, and Arrow were sitting. Even though there were enough chairs, Romeo sat down with me in his lap.

"You don't want to join the battle?" I asked the group as he signaled to one of the bartenders.

"I prefer to eat dinner dry," Hopper mused.

"I'm starving," Arrow announced.

A bartender appeared wearing a relaxed cream-colored linen short set. He placed a beer in front of my husband and turned to our once-blond friend. Arrow had stopped bleaching his hair about a year after he retired from racing. Just showed up at one of our family get-togethers with a buzzcut.

Since then, his hair had grown into a messy brown mop that flipped out around his ears. Even fifteen years later, he still had a baby face. And honestly, I still secretly thought he looked like Justin Bieber.

"Please help yourself to the buffet," the bartender told Arrow, gesturing to the massive spread. "All the food is prepared and ready to be enjoyed."

"Thank you," he said.

Lorhaven caught the bartender's attention to order a beer for him and a daiquiri for Joey.

When the man was gone, Arrow pressed his palms onto the arms of his chair and stood. He'd filled out over the years, becoming wider, and both his arms were covered in full sleeves of tattoos. The loose tank top he wore showed them off perfectly as well as offering glimpses of a few on his chest.

He stood and turned toward the pool where half the family was still trying to drown each other. Placing fingers between his lips, he whistled.

Everyone looked around, and he waved. "Let's eat!"

I glanced at Hopper, and he winked at me. "Better feed him before he gets hangry."

Hopper's dark hair seemed curlier than usual, likely from the salt and humidity on the island, and the breeze ruffled it around his forehead. He, too, was more tattooed than he used to be, but Arrow would always have more ink than anyone else here.

Hopper laid a hand on the back of his husband's neck and directed him toward the food.

"So, Rimmel, how are the shelters?"

I turned back to Joey who had her dark curly hair piled on top of her head. A pair of sunglasses pushed up kept the loose strands away from her green eyes. Her flawless skin seemed golden in the island light across her neck and shoulders, which were bare above her strapless maxi dress.

I ran three shelters now. Well, I owned three and had a lot of help running them. My main focus was still the one I took over when it was first built.

"They're doing great," I said. "We just hired a veterinarian at the new location. It's going to be a clinic as well as a shelter."

Romeo's arm tightened around me from behind. "You do a lot of good work, baby."

Lorhaven smiled. "How many dogs do you have at home right now?"

I laughed. "Just a few."

"Lies!" Braeden appeared, soaking wet and missing his shirt. He came close and shook himself, splattering Romeo and me with water.

"Braeden," I shrieked, crawling farther against Romeo.

"I had to do it, sis. I need to cool off your lies," he deadpanned, sticking a finger in his ear like he needed to drain it.

Pushing his wet hair back, Braeden turned to Lorhaven. "Ten," he said. "Ten dogs, which ain't just a few."

"You like my dogs," I told him.

"I like you, so I tolerate those dogs." He corrected me.

"You take Milo and Rocket to football practice with you every afternoon," I refuted. Every day, he whistled, and every day, those two dogs tripped over themselves jumping up into the cab of his truck.

"The kids like them." He defended himself.

Romeo laughed.

Braeden gave him the finger.

"How's your father?" I asked Joey about Ron Gamble, the owner of the Maryland Knights. "We were sorry to hear he couldn't join us."

Lorhaven made a sound. "Man is pushing eighty, and he's still a workaholic."

"That's never going to change." Joey agreed. "But he's doing good. Set in his ways. He sends his regards, Romeo. Wants to have dinner when we get home."

Romeo nodded. "He called me. We'll be there."

"Rome's his favorite football player," Braeden put in.

"Rome made Gamble a lot of money over the years. Instead of being filthy rich, now he's obscenely rich," Lorhaven said of his father-in-law.

Trent's wet feet slapped over the concrete, alerting us to his presence. Like Braeden, he shook his sandy-brown hair all over, making it rain.

"Ugh!" I exclaimed. "Not you too!"

Laughing, Trent shook his hair out one last time, then peeled the T-shirt over his head and dropped it on the ground. He still worked for New Revolution Racing on the business side, but having an office-type job didn't make him soft. If anything, it made him hit the gym harder, and he was just as big as always.

"Sorry, sis," he said, leaning over Romeo and me to smack a wet kiss on my temple. "I still love ya."

I sighed. I was a total sucker for my brothers.

Drew appeared, his soaked hair plastered to his head, water dripping from his scruff, and blue eyes narrowed.

Crossing his arms over his chest, he scrutinized Trent. "Where is your shirt?"

Trent smirked. "Figured I'd eat without one tonight."

Drew growled. "Oh, hells no."

"What's going on?" Arrow asked, his lips smacking as he chewed and his hands filled with loaded-down plates.

"Drew's got his panties in a wad as usual," Lorhaven cracked.

"Maybe you should put on a shirt," Hopper told Trent.

Arrow sat down and started plowing through a mound of food. Appreciative noises fell from his lips. "This is damn good."

The bartender delivered Joey's and Lorhaven's drinks.

"Isn't anyone else going to eat?" Arrow asked, pausing midchew.

Drew slapped him on the shoulder. "I'm going now before you eat it all."

Travis appeared, black hair mashed to his head and the black jeans he always lived in soaked. Like his dad, his shirt was missing.

"This pig is delicious," he said, shoveling a huge bite of meat between his lips.

My nose wrinkled.

"Where is your plate?" Ivy exclaimed, coming over to plant her hands on her hips and scold her nephew. "I know you did not go over there to the carving station and hold out your hand for a slab of meat."

She was the only one who took the time after being dumped in the pool to comb out her long blond locks and exchange her wet clothes for a one-piece shorts romper that tied in a big bow at the back of her neck. She would always be this family's best dressed.

Travis shoved more in his mouth. "He gave it to me," he said, defending his poor manners.

"It's so good," Arrow moaned, shoving some in his mouth.

Travis and Arrow high-fived over the table.

Ivy grabbed Travis by the ear. "No nephew of mine is going to be walking around with handfuls of meat."

"Ow, Aunt Ivy!" Travis complained.

"We're getting a plate." Exasperated and still gripping his ear, Ivy turned to Trent and Drew. "Really? Is this what you taught your son?"

"He's a growing boy." Drew defended them.

Jax appeared with meat in his hand too. "I've never seen a pig roast before," he told everyone, taking a huge bite.

"You have got to be kidding!" Ivy exclaimed, throwing up her hands.

Everyone laughed.

Jax looked at Braeden. "What?"

Valerie, Tony, Caroline, and John came around the path leading to the clubhouse. All four of them looked far more put together than the rest of us. The second Valerie saw the meat in the boys' hands, her nose wrinkled.

"We use plates in this family, boys," she told them. "Come on. Let's go."

"I've tried," Ivy implored to Caroline.

Caroline patted her daughter-in-law on the shoulder. "You're a good mom, honey. They get this from their fathers."

"I'm literally your son and standing right here," Braeden deadpanned.

Caroline laughed and patted his cheek before going off to help Valerie give the boys a lesson in manners.

The other kids came up from the beach, and the entire family moved to the buffet to fill plates and sit down at a row of tables all pushed together. Palm trees swayed in the night breeze, light glowed from lanterns and tiki torches, and music played over speakers I couldn't see.

Drinks flowed, and laughter filled the air.

The sun disappeared completely, and the sky turned velvet, filling with more stars than I'd ever seen before.

Stomach and heart full, I laid my head against Romeo's shoulder and gazed up at the glittering night. The sound of the ocean lulled me, and the warmth of my husband made me feel safe.

Romeo nuzzled into my hair, his nose nudging the side of my neck. "Is it later yet?" he whispered, causing goose bumps to rise along my bare arms.

I wiggled in his lap, and he growled deep in his throat.

"How about we call it a night?" he murmured.

I started to nod, but a sizzling sound followed by clapping brought up my head.

One of the staff held open the door of the clubhouse while several others came out. They were clapping and smiling, and behind them, a cart was pushed out with a massive white cake in the center. A few sparklers stuck out of the top, shooting off sparks in all directions.

"Happy retirement, Rome!" Braeden yelled, rising from his chair.

Romeo laughed and stood, setting me on my feet beside him. The cake was wheeled to the head of the table, and Braeden slung his arm around Romeo's shoulders, guiding him over.

"Speech!" Trent yelled.

Everyone followed suit and started to chant. *"Speech, speech, speech!"*

Romeo shook his head, his smile blinding even against the backdrop of paradise. He and Braeden stood behind the cake until the sparklers burned out and the staff retreated inside.

The bartenders carried over trays of champagne glasses filled with bubbly and began passing them out to the adults.

"We know you're a man of few words, Rome," Braeden

said. "But we did drag ourselves across the globe for this. So how about you say something?"

Romeo's gaze met mine across the table, and I smiled.

He cleared his throat and looked around the massive table with our entire family filling it. His golden hair glowed against the moon and torches, candlelight flickering in his blue eyes. With a gauzy white button-up shirt hugging his shoulders and billowing around his narrow waist and the champagne flute in his large hand, he looked very much like the head of the family. A true alpha who wrote his own rules, loved with everything he was made of, and built a family that not even DNA could rival.

We all played our part in this family. We were all the heroes of our individual stories, but Romeo—my Romeo—he was where it all began.

"Well, since you all dragged yourselves across the globe," he mused.

Everyone heckled but then fell quiet as Romeo's chest rose and fell.

"You know, when I was young—"

"Old man!" Alex called, and everyone laughed.

"I always thought—*planned*—that football would be my biggest accomplishment. The best thing I would ever do." His eyes connected with mine again, and the tether we created all those years ago tugged my heart. Smiling, he shifted his glance to his parents. "And you both made sure I had all the opportunity and support I needed to realize those dreams."

Valerie smiled and dabbed the corner of her eye with a napkin.

"I know I wouldn't have made it as far as I did without you both, so thank you for that, Mom, Dad." He lifted his glass in a small salute.

"But here I stand fifteen years later with what I thought would be my biggest accomplishment in the rearview mirror. Don't get me wrong. I love football. I love the game. And yeah, maybe I set a record or two."

Trent coughed. "More like six."

Romeo grinned. "Won a few Super Bowls."

Liam coughed. "Eight."

"What can I say? I'm a legend," Romeo allowed, smug and big-headed as always.

But it was okay. He'd earned it for tonight.

"But as I stand here tonight with all those accomplishments under my belt and fifteen years of playing to ruminate on..." He paused and gazed out across the ocean. As he turned back, his Adam's apple bobbed, and he smiled. "I can honestly say football is not my biggest accomplishment." His stare found mine and held. "This is."

"Grandpa's going soft!" Arrow called.

"What's wrong with being a grandpa?" Anthony retorted.

Romeo shook his head. "At the risk of sounding like an after-school special—"

"What's an after-school special?" Blue asked, and Romeo groaned.

"All that time I was playing, something else became bigger. We built something better. Life became about way more than me and a ball. And maybe if football was all I had all these years, then yeah, retirement might be bitter. But looking around this massive table that B so generously paid for—"

"I'll never quit you, Rome," B called.

"This family we built, the unshakable relationships and loyalty we've all worked hard to form and keep... This is my biggest accomplishment. *Our* accomplishment. And though the expiration date on my football career has been reached, this family is forever."

Romeo raised his glass higher. "Thanks for being here to

celebrate my retirement, but let's also celebrate this fam because, in the end, there's nothing better."

Glasses rose.

"To family!"

Everyone echoed Romeo's sentiment, and we all sipped from our drinks.

"That was corny as hell, Rome," Braeden teased after finishing off his champagne. He turned to the table. "Who wants cake?"

Romeo grabbed the back of his head. "Well, since you paid, it's only fair you have the first piece," he quipped and pushed his face into the massive white confection.

Braeden yanked himself back, vanilla cake and white icing covering his entire face and hairline. Using his fingers, he swiped it out of his eyes and then swiped his tongue across the corner of his mouth.

"This is pretty good," he said, then grabbed a fistful and launched it at Romeo's head.

They ended up locked in a wrestling match, and Braeden stepped on a mound of icing and went flying backward. Romeo tried to catch him, but he ended up toppling over too, and both men fell into the rolling cart and hit the ground, the cake tumbling over on top of them.

Heavy silence draped over the group, and I hurried around the table to stand by Ivy and gape at the overgrown children we called husbands. They were in a heap on their backs, cake literally everywhere and covering them both.

Braeden groaned and pushed up onto his elbow, a chunk of cake rolling off his head. Romeo sat up, cake on his shoulder and icing dangling from his ear. His hair was no longer golden but frosted.

"This is why our sons don't use plates," Ivy deadpanned.

I laughed.

"You were right, B. This cake is pretty good," Romeo said, swiping some off his arm to eat.

"Right?" Braeden said, licking his arm.

"So much for cake," Arrow mourned.

Joey laughed. "They just brought out a tray of cupcakes."

Arrow ran off, and all the kids followed him.

Romeo leaped up from the mess and scooped me into his arms, making me squeal.

"Roman Anderson! You're sticky!"

"I've come to give you some sugar," he said, pressing our lips together and smearing icing all over the lower half of my face.

I started to protest, but his tongue slipped between my lips and, with it, the sweet taste of vanilla frosting. Sighing, I gave in, as I always did, to this man and kissed him back.

Nearby, Valerie cleared her throat. I pulled back, dipping my face into Romeo's chest.

"Well, hopefully you boys have gotten all of these antics out of your systems on the first day so we can have a more… relaxed vacation."

"They're heathens, Mrs. Anderson," Ivy declared. "I've lost hope."

"Valerie." Romeo's mom corrected Ivy and then laughed.

Braeden stood in the center of the pile of cake. "Don't worry, Moms," he said, glancing at her and then at his mother. "Yoga class starts at seven a.m. by the pool."

"Oh, how lovely," Caroline said.

"I'll be in bed," he told her. "Enjoy it, though."

"London will enjoy that," Valerie said, glancing at me.

I nodded. "I'll tell all the girls."

"We will be sure to keep an eye on them," Caroline told me. "That way you can sleep in after all that travel."

"Oh, well, this is your vacation too. I don't expect you to babysit our kids."

"Please, this Gram can't sleep past sunrise no matter the day. Yoga with my granddaughters is the perfect start to my day," Caroline refuted.

"Me too," Valerie said. "We can have breakfast with a view afterward."

"Well, if you're sure…" I hedged.

"Of course we are." Both women nodded.

Valerie laid her hand on mine, then drew back when she felt the icing coating my skin. "Enjoy your time with your husband. I know we are celebrating his retirement, but it's yours too. Being the wife of a famous pro football player for fifteen years also deserves recognition." She paused. "Not that I think that's all you are," she rushed to say, forgoing her aversion to my sticky hand and reaching for it once more. "You are a wonderful mother, business owner, philanthropist, and daughter as well. I just meant—"

I laid my free hand over hers, stopping her rambling. "I know, Mom."

Valerie's eyes widened, lips parting in surprise. She searched my face almost as if she couldn't believe I'd willingly called her mom.

I smiled. "I know what you meant, and thank you for saying it. I couldn't have accomplished everything I have without your and Anthony's help. You've been amazing grandparents to our children and amazing parents to Romeo… and to me."

"Rimmel," Valerie practically gasped. Tears filled her eyes.

"I know I don't say it, but I do love you."

A cry ripped from her lips, and she pulled me in for a hug. "Oh, honey, I never thought I'd hear you say that."

"Never underestimate this family," I whispered.

"We love you too," Valerie confided.

After fifteen years, I could honestly say that the rough start Valerie Anderson and I got off to was firmly behind us.

Her love for my children, my husband… and yeah, me was just water under the bridge we now stood on.

Nearby, Romeo cleared his throat.

I pulled away from Valerie and looked at him.

"I have cake in my ear," he complained.

"Serves you right for wrestling like that with Braeden. And at family dinner!"

"Honestly, Roman," Valerie scolded. "Go shower."

"C'mon, smalls," Romeo said, holding out his hand.

"Me? Why do I have to come?"

"Because if I leave you alone, you'll get lost at sea."

"How could that happen with the bright yellow and orange vests everyone keeps handing me?" I sassed.

Swooping in, he picked me up, dumping me over his shoulder like a sack of potatoes.

"Put me down!"

"Can't do it," he said, heading off toward our room. "Look at that. Now you're covered in cake and need a shower too."

He smeared his gross hand along the back of my thigh.

"You're going to pay for this!" I vowed, my body dangling down his back.

"Oh, sweetheart, I'm counting on it."

10

ROMEO

DO ME A SOLID AND KEEP MY KIDS BUSY FOR AN HOUR, I TEXTED Trent after washing all the cake out of my ears.

His reply was nearly instant. *I'll make it two.*

He was a good brother. A good dad and uncle too.

Smiling, I tossed the cell on the lounge chair by the wide-open doors leading out onto the deck where my wife was sitting, legs folded beneath her and a towel draped around her back. Lying on the deck beside her was a hairbrush that she'd used to comb through her wet shoulder-length locks.

Not willing to waste one minute of our two-hour alone time, I strolled out across the deck, naked as the day I was born. Everyone was at the clubhouse, and the only thing around us was ocean. With the sun down and the moon in the sky, the air was cooler than earlier in the day but still too balmy to be considered cold.

I sank behind Rim, spreading my legs to fit her between

my thighs. She sighed and leaned into my chest, surren-
dering all her weight.

Humming, I tugged the edge of the towel off her shoulder
and brushed her hair out of the way to kiss across her skin
and lick up her neck. Her head tilted, and she reached for my
hand, threading our fingers together.

I continued kissing across her freshly washed skin, the
faint taste of ocean painting my tongue. Her small ass
wiggled back, fitting deeper against me and turning my semi
into a full-on raging hard-on.

"I will never have enough of you," I whispered against her
ear before tugging the lobe between my lips.

She whimpered, moving our clasped hands beneath the
towel to press them against her bare waist.

"Mrs. Anderson," I rumbled, caressing her skin. "Are you
naked out here on this deck?"

"It's later, Romeo." She beckoned me.

Untangling my fingers from hers, my palm slid over her
breast to massage her supple skin. Her nipple hardened
instantly, and I rolled it between two fingers, plucking until
it was puckered tight.

Rimmel craned her head, and I lowered mine, claiming
her mouth in an ardent kiss. Hunching around her, the pressure of my hands increased, rubbing her breasts and waist as
my tongue twirled with hers until there was no separation.

Boldly, she sucked my lower lip into her mouth, the sweet
pressure of her enthusiasm had my dick rocking against her
hip as my hand fell away from her breast, dragging down to
the center of her body.

We both groaned, her mouth unlatching from my lip as
she shuddered in pleasure. Without hesitation, I dipped two
fingers right into her silky heat and swirled them around.

Her legs trembled as I pushed in and out of her core, her

body arching against mine as her hands clung to any part of me she could grab.

Waves lapped against the deck, the balmy breeze wrapped around us, and lust turned me blind to everything else.

Groaning, I slipped my fingers from her body, dragging them up her middle, leaving a trail of wetness between her breasts as I continued to her mouth.

Her lips parted the moment I reached her chin, and I pushed those two digits drenched in her desire against her tongue. She sucked instantly, and my dick jumped just imagining that hot little tongue swirling around my tip.

"Does that taste good, baby?" I wanted to know.

Her head bobbed as she sucked me even deeper.

I moved restlessly, and she pulled back, tossing the towel from between us and turning around so she could straddle my lap.

My rigid dick poked her instantly, the breath whooshing out of my lungs the second her slick core greeted my swollen head.

She gasped. "Mr. Anderson. Are you naked out here on this deck?"

"Sit on my dick, Rimmel," I growled, far too impatient for more teasing. "Right now."

My head fell back when her body sheathed mine, snug walls silky and warm as she pushed down and stretched to accommodate my girth.

Fingers twisting gently in my damp hair, she pulled my head down, and I blinked open my eyes to stare at her ever-beautiful face. "You feel so good," I told her.

Wrapping her arms around my neck, she pressed our chests together and planted her chin on my shoulder. I held her as tight as I dared, hoping to imprint her shape on mine as I rocked up into her, burrowing deep into her core.

We swayed together, our bodies straining, her fingertips

biting into the muscles of my back as she ground down on my lap with wild abandon. Pleasure built, pressure and desperation spilled over, and I pushed up, taking her with me and striding through the open sliders and to the king-sized bed made up in white.

It was slightly cooler inside, sheer white curtains billowing in the ocean air. The only light was from the moon over the ocean, the pristine white covering on the bed a beacon for our bodies.

I laid my wife out across the mattress and kneeled between her legs.

"Wider," I rasped and felt insane satisfaction when she spread her thighs farther.

Feeling possessive and greedy, I laid my palms against her legs and pushed them wider, opening her up until I could see it all. Pinning her down, I lowered, licking right up her slit, which was open and wet.

We both groaned, and I dived in, practically suffocating myself with her body, using her as my only oxygen. She trembled and whispered my name, straining against the bed as I availed myself of her taste.

Her frame went rigid, and I felt her waist arch. She fought against it, but I doubled down. "Give it to me, baby," I said, spearing her with my tongue and fingers.

She shattered against my tongue, her body spasming as she came and her moans echoing to the ceiling. Her hands twisted in the covers as she bucked, and I kept going, sucking and licking until she collapsed against the sheets in a boneless heap.

Licking softly, I drew back, pressing a few sloppy kisses on the inside of her thigh.

Panting, she stared down at me, her brown eyes glittering in the night. "My turn."

A thrill shot down my spine, tingling my lower back and

making me smile with anticipation. I shot to my knees as she sat up. Grabbing my hips, she pulled herself closer, fitting her body between my spread knees and swallowing my dick like the pro she was.

This woman knew exactly how to work me over, the perfect angle to twirl her tongue, and the exact right amount of pressure to suck. Nails digging into my bare hips, she pushed deeper, taking me past her gag reflex until my engorged head hit the back of her throat.

I groaned, pushing a little deeper as her fingers curled into my crack, encouraging me to use her more. I nudged my head against the silky skin of her throat, and she hummed, the slight vibration making tingles race across my back.

Worrying it was too much, I began easing off, but she made a sound of protest and pulled me back, swallowing around my rod and making me shudder. My fingers dug into her shoulder, and she swallowed again before slowly, torturously dragging down my rod until her lips rested against the tip.

Panting, I looked down, finding her wide eyes already staring up at me, her expression far away and wrecked.

Swiping my thumb over her cheekbone, I unleashed the full weight of my love for her in my eyes. "I said it years ago, and I'll say it right now. I'll say it in another ten years and then another after that. You, Rimmel, you are my once-in-a-lifetime. My greatest love, my favorite girl, and my biggest accomplishment."

"Oh, Romeo…"

She could sigh my name a million more times and it would never get old.

"You're my greatest love too. Always."

I pushed her down and thrust into her, our cries mingling with the sounds of the ocean as I claimed her again and again. Her body molded to mine, fitting together like two halves of a single whole. Pleasure rode me hard, everything reducing to the feel of her clenching around me and the soft sound of our skin slapping.

Release built inside me, tightening my stomach and drawing up my balls. My fingers curled into the sheets as I thrust and groaned.

"Come for me again, baby. Come all over my cock."

She wrapped her legs around my hips, and I thrust deep, holding myself still so she could rock and rub against me.

She cried out, and the dam inside me broke. I threw my head back, a deep guttural groan ripping out of me to echo around the room. My dick convulsed inside her, my release emptying into her body, claiming her from the inside out.

I continued to thrust, pushing as deep as I could as aftershocks sparked like lightning down my spine. Completely spent, I dropped onto the bed, rolling us so she was on top of me. Her cheek pressed against my sweat-slicked chest, and she sighed heavily.

"You still got it," she mused.

I laughed. "Don't you forget it."

"Like you'd let me."

I grinned up to the ceiling. "If I still got it, it's because you inspire it in me."

"Flattery will get you everywhere," she sang.

"I don't need to go anywhere, baby. I'm already where I want to be."

Lifting her head, she pressed a kiss over my heart.

We lay there in comfortable silence for long moments with me pulling my fingers through her damp hair. "I got you a present."

She snorted and propped her chin on my chest to look at me. "Yes, Romeo. Your cock is a present."

I threw back my head and laughed. "I like the way you think."

Her eyes rolled. "I've been with you for more than fifteen years. I know exactly how your mind works."

Chuckling, I shimmied out from beneath her, and she flopped on the bed.

"Hey, where are you going?"

I reached into the dresser across the room and pulled out a white velvet box. "So you were expecting this, then?"

Her face softened as she pushed into a sitting position, her beautiful body unabashedly on display. "I never expect things with you, Romeo. You exceed any expectation I could ever dream up."

My heart somersaulted, and I carried the gift over. "In that case, this is for you."

Every time I gave her a gift, her hands fluttered around it almost as if it were too precious to just reach out and grab. And every time she did it, something in me loved her a little more.

I had no idea how this woman managed to find so much love in me, but it seemed when it came to her, it was boundless.

"It's your retirement. Why would you get me a gift?"

I shook my head. "It's not just my retirement, baby. It's ours. You sacrificed and gave a lot for me to have the career I did." I hesitated, old and familiar doubts rearing their heads. I shook free of them, not wanting them to encroach on her moment. "Everyone might be celebrating me, but you are the one who made this possible."

"That was all you, Romeo."

"No." I was swift and decisive, climbing onto the bed to mirror her position. "I know as sure and steady as my heartbeat that the main reason I made it all the way to the golden age of fifteen in football is because of you and the support you gave without fail."

She started to shake her head, but I leaned in, grasping

her face and holding it in my palms. "You picked up a lot of slack. You traveled. Dealt with tired, whiny kids. School projects, parent conferences, football practices. Suffered through constant, scrupulous, and mean media attention. Rabid fans."

"Bobble-headed Barbies," she muttered, wrinkling her cute nose.

Ah, I love that she still gets jealous.

"Watched me get sacked, worried over my injuries, fed me, washed my laundry, put up with too much time away—"

Her fingers pressed against my lips, silencing my tirade. "I'd do it all again a million times over. It's not a sacrifice when it's for someone I love. For you."

"Open the box," I said, gruff.

She always said I had the pretty words, but hers always hit the hardest.

She smiled when I pushed it toward her and then sighed as her hands finally settled around it. "It's soft," she whispered, rubbing her palm over the white fabric.

The tiny hinges were silent as she lifted the lid, her small gasp audible even against my thundering heart. I was nervous.

This woman made me nervous.

I just wanted so badly to make her happy. To make sure she understood just how much of me she owned. I never wanted her to feel like she'd settled. That she'd traded something for me. For our life.

"Romeo..." Her voice quivered, fingers doing that fluttering thing again over the inside of the box. "This is... *gorgeous.*"

Something in me relaxed, the reverence in her voice all I needed to hear.

Her fingers continued to hover before pressing against her throat. "It's..."

"Our legacy." I finished. "Yours and mine."

Tears spilled over her cheeks, and she swiped at them furiously. "Oh, don't let me make it a mess." She worried.

Using my thumbs, I dried her cheeks and then reached for the necklace she'd yet to touch.

"Where did you get this?" she asked.

"I had it made. Just for you," I explained, palming the brooch-like pendant in my palm. It was oval and similar in size to the pendant she loved so much that once belonged to her mother.

"The chain is diamond cut, so its extra strong for a little hazard like you," I teased, and she smiled.

The tip of her finger caressed the large oval stone making up the pendant. "What is this?"

"White rainbow moonstone," I answered, tilting it a little so she could see the various colors. It looked like an opal to me, a milky-white stone with ribbons of color throughout. There were pink, peach, gray, and blue with hints of green. Under certain lights, there was yellow... It was endlessly a new color to be found in every new light.

"It's set in twenty-four-carat gold," I explained, showing her the flat back that would rest against her skin.

"And the tree," she whispered, still studying it like it deserved all her concentration.

"It's handmade of gold too," I confirmed, taking in the single tree, our family tree, covering the center. It had a sturdy trunk with many strong branches reaching out to the golden edge. The moonstone behind it looked sort of like the sky.

On the end of the branches were a few stones. Seven of them to be exact. The birthstone of each of our four kids along with hers and mine.

"I meant what I said at dinner. This family, *our* family, will forever be our greatest legacy."

She fell into me, crying against my shoulder, wiping her snot and tears all over my freshly showered chest. "I swear, Roman Anderson, you are too good to be true."

She was good for my ego.

Pulling her back, I tipped up her chin. "It is true. It's right here on our family tree."

She took the necklace then. The sight of it in her palm was so right. "Romeo?"

"Hmm?"

"There's an extra birthstone." She pointed out a black diamond on one of the branches. "Whose is this?"

"You don't know?" I teased.

"If I knew, I wouldn't ask!"

Teasing her would never get old. "It's Murphy's."

Her eyes widened. "Murphy?"

"Mmm," I hummed, tucking her hair behind her ear. "He was sort of our first son, right? Couldn't leave him out."

And she started crying again. Loud, shoulder-wracking sobs. "Murphy," she wailed, flopping into me again.

I held her tight, letting her snot all over me and smiling while it happened.

I missed that cat. He'd lived a long, healthy life, and to this day, I still thought he was a big part of me winning Rimmel back after all the shit hit the fan. He was there from the beginning, and even though he wasn't here in body anymore, his spirit was. And so were his ashes that sat on our mantel beside his photo.

"I miss him." Rimmel sniffled after her weeping subsided.

"Well, now he's right here." I tapped the hand holding the necklace.

"How did you know his birthstone?" She wondered, sitting back. Strands of hair stuck to her wet cheeks, and the tip of her nose was red. "We never knew his birthday."

I shrugged. "I didn't. I picked black because that's what color he was."

"It's perfect," she whispered, hugging the pendant against her heart. "I love it more than anything."

"It's gotta go back."

Her head whipped up. "What?"

"I'm glad you like it sweetheart, but I can't have it around if you love it more than me."

"You gave it to me. That's why I can love it so much."

I pursed my lips. "I'll allow it."

She thrust it at me. "Help me put it on?"

I clasped it around her neck, gently settling the pendant against her chest.

"Oh, it's just too precious to wear. But how can I take it off?"

"It's made to wear, baby. That's why I bought it." And made sure it was enforced. And insured. And the design was saved in case I had to have it remade.

Look, I loved my wife, but we all knew she was constantly three seconds away from some sort of disaster.

"I'll treasure it," she whispered, laying her hand over it. "Thank you, Romeo."

I kissed the tip of her nose, crusty with snot.

She popped up, suddenly filled with energy, and bounded off the bed, nearly falling on her ass.

"Rimmel," I warned.

She laughed and raced into the walk-in closet attached to our room. I heard the zipper on a suitcase, and then she was bounding back onto the bed, the mattress barely bouncing beneath her weight.

"I got you something too!" she said, eyes bright.

I arched an eyebrow. "You did?"

She turned shy. "Well, it's not a private island and a family reunion," she said, waving her hand around the room.

"It's probably better."

She glanced down at the box wrapped in purple and fingered the slightly crooked gold bow on the top. "It got a little smooshed in the suitcase."

Leaning in, I kissed her forehead. "Thanks for the gift, baby."

She pushed it into my lap. "Open it."

After ripping away the wrapping, I pulled the lid off the box and reached into the tissue paper to pull out a leather-bound book.

"My little #nerd," I teased. "Got me a book."

"Well, if you don't want it…" she sang, reaching to take it away.

I pulled it into my chest, wrapping my arms around it. "Better watch yourself, smalls."

Not intimidated in the least, she climbed right into my lap. Laughing beneath my breath, I wrapped my arms around her, holding the book in front of us so I could look at it.

The book was bound in brown leather, the same kind footballs were made of. The spine had white leather laces, and the front was embossed with gold foil lettering.

FOOTBALL HISTORY of ROMEO ANDERSON
MARYLAND KNIGHTS
ALPHA U WOLVES

"It's not just a book," she said. "It's *your* book."

I caressed the leather, gently rubbed the shiny letters, and traced over the golden football toward the bottom.

"Ever since we started dating, I've been collecting things. Photographs, articles that have been printed, even a few of the early notifications from the dreaded #Buzzboss. When you signed with the Knights and all the years after."

Surprised, I stared down at my wife. "You have?"

Her dark head bobbed, and she opened the cover to show me the inside. "Of course. You love football. It's your dream. And you are so good at it, the greatest quarterback to ever play."

"That might be a stretch," I mused.

"Not to me." She was definitive. Her fingers tapped on the pages, and I glanced down and started to flip through.

It really was *my* book.

Flabbergasted, I stared at page after page filled with moments from my entire career, starting at Alpha U and going through the entire fifteen years I'd played for the Knights. Just as she said, there were headlines, news stories, stats, and recountings of every record I set. There were professional photos and personal ones I knew she took herself. There were pics of me on the field with the kids and, hell, photos from when I'd proposed to her in the middle of a game.

"It's all here," I said, completely amazed. "My entire career."

Leaning farther into my chest, she reached back to anchor her hand at the nape of my neck. "Oh no, I could never fit your entire amazing career inside one book. But I put as much as I could, the highlights and even some of the struggles. It's a record of your achievements, the story of your love and commitment to the game. I wanted you to have this so you could look at it anytime and remember just how incredible you are."

Groaning, I left the book in her lap and wrapped around her from behind. Pressing my face against her neck, I breathed deep, overcome with emotion. "I can't believe you did this. This must have taken forever."

"Fifteen years in the making." She agreed. "But it was worth it. You are the kind of man books are written about. But I didn't write this book. You did. I just collected it all and had it made into this.

Sniffling a little, I put my chin on her shoulder, and we flipped through the rest together. When we were done, my chest was tight and my eyes were misty. I made it. *We* made it.

"Thank you," I whispered, kissing her cheek. "For making this. For being my biggest fan."

"Always," she echoed.

"I love it. And I love you."

She lifted her chin, and I kissed her. Against her lips, I smiled, "I think it beats the private island vacay."

She giggled, then turned thoughtful. "How much do you think this cost Braeden anyway?"

"Two mil, easy."

Gasping, she fell back on her butt, then toppled over the rest of the way. "Two million dollars!"

I reached over and grabbed her bare ass to give it a squeeze.

She squealed.

"Now we know why B did that insurance commercial."

She sat up. "The one with the talking duck?"

I laughed. "That'd be the one. Never thought I'd see the day the Hulk was talking to a freaking duck on national TV about insurance."

Her eyes rounded. "You think he did that to pay for this?"

"Seems like something he would do," I mused. And I knew damn well all these sponsorships and endorsements paid crazy amounts of money. Hell, I'd just done a campaign with a major brand that paid twice that.

Her teeth sank into her lower lip, and I saw her begin to worry.

"Hey," I said, catching her chin to look into her eyes. "You know we can afford this, right? Braeden too. I'd never let him drop this kinda cash if I thought it would put a hardship on him and Ivy in any way."

Her eyes cleared, and she nodded. "I know. Ivy makes a lot too. I mean, she has a TV show."

"I still can't believe she has an entire TV show based on giving people makeovers."

"She's so good at it. Everyone wants to be styled by Ivy." Rimmel defended.

"I know," I mused. "Princess has done well for herself." Between the YouTube channel, presence in *People* magazine, styling a few A-list celebrities and now everyone on national TV, the girl was fashion royalty.

I was proud of her. She worked hard. Her and B both.

That feeling I shook off earlier tapped the base of my spine, telling me it was still there. "Rim?"

"Hmm?" she said, fingers gently tracing the tree in the center of the new pendant.

"Can I ask you something?"

Hearing the serious note in my voice, she looked up, giving me her complete attention. "Anything."

"Tell me the truth."

Her brows furrowed, but she nodded.

"Do you have regrets?"

Surprise flashed over her features. "Regrets?"

"That you didn't go to vet school like you wanted when we met. Do you feel like you missed out on something because of… me?"

She gasped. It was hella dramatic and moved her entire body. "Oh my god, Romeo! Is that what you think?"

"I don't think it," I echoed. "But sometimes I worry."

She gasped again, falling over with it this time. She was completely ridiculous. But she was naked, so it was okay.

The blankets tugged as she scrambled up, then dove into my lap, wrapping her body around mine to cling like a koala.

"Eyes on me, Roman Anderson."

I choked at her demand.

Her small, cool fingers found my chin and pulled it down, doing to me what I had done so many times to her. Our eyes collided, and hers were fierce and unflinching, resolve in their depths.

"Now you listen to me," she said, squeezing my chin. "I have never, not once, not even for a fraction of a millisecond ever regretted a moment with you. Or any decision I ever made. I told you all those years ago that my dream changed. My dream was you and this family… our kids. You gave me all of that and so much more. I might not be a veterinarian, but we have three clinics that do so much good and keep me so busy. There isn't any room in my life for anything to be missing because it is so full, and the reason it's so full is all because of you."

Well. I felt better.

"I love this life. *You.*" Her hand wrapped around the pendant. "Our legacy."

I kissed her then. Long and languid until my lungs screamed for air and spots started to float behind my eyelids. Her hands were everywhere, in my hair, gripping my ears, and scratching a path down the length of my back. I flipped her onto her back and thrust deep, the warm silk of her body welcoming me home.

"Fifteen years of loving you," I told her. "But our legacy is far from over, baby. Because you and me? This fam? We're an entire lifetime."

An entire lifetime of #love.

The End

AUTHOR'S NOTE

A DECADE OF #HASHTAG

When I wrote *#Nerd* in 2014, I never imagined—not even once—that I would be sitting here ten years later writing this. I never imagined *#Nerd* would have an e-book, paperback, hardback, a one-year anniversary hardback, an audiobook, an alternate paperback, a special edition paperback, a cinematic book trailer, *and* also be published in French and Italian. There's also a *Hashtag* coloring book! LOL

And now, the ten-year anniversary hardback edition and this little update that turned into a novella. *#Fam.*

I mean, wow. That doesn't even include all the awards it's won! That's a lot considering I just wanted to write a book with a boy inspired by Paul Walker and my love of 90's movies.

And that one book turned into an entire series (with a spinoff series!) that has been loved and never forgotten by all of you. I mean, if I had to define success, I would say this right here is it. The love for *#Nerd* and the rest of *Hashtag* has basically shaped my entire career. I did have well-loved books before *#Nerd,* but this was on a different level. The way you all have loved Romeo and Rimmel still surprises me ten years later. You all have kept this series alive over an entire decade, and for that I have to #ThankYou. Thank you for helping bring it to another generation of readers.

I will admit it's a bit intimidating, and over the last ten years, I have often wondered if I would ever write anything that is loved like *Hashtag* again. I have often worried no one would want a book from me without a # in front of it. You all have proved time and again that you will read a book of mine without a #, and it warms my writer heart.

It's been ten years of really great experiences because of *#Nerd*—going to book events and having long lines and seeing my book brought to life with an epic book trailer. Winning awards and being recognized for writing. Having people wear the Romeo hoodie religiously and dress up like Rimmel for character-themed parties. The hashtag #Wheres-Romeo filled my reader group for so long with readers posting pics of lime-green Hellcats. And I must mention the #ZachMustDie hashtag when our resident villain was wreaking havoc on our favorite fam.

There have been a few rough times as well in the decade of *Hashtag*. The well-known and loved model for Romeo—Nathan Weller—who appears in the book trailer, on the cover of the one-year anniversary edition, *#Heart*, *#Holiday*, and *#Bae*, passed away unexpectedly. Over the years, he'd attended many signings with me, and we'd become friends. His passing was a hard blow for me and for readers who knew him as Romeo. He might not be here anymore, but to me, he will always be Romeo.

Many have asked for a movie or TV show. To that, I will disclose that I came close to the possibility of a TV show, but the option agreement fell through. We (me and my former agent) did try for many, many years, but alas, it hasn't worked out. Maybe someday.

Readers still ask for more books in this series—especially

a series for the kids—which I always say is a possibility! That also is a bit intimidating for me because I feel the pressure to make the kids' series just as good as the original, but can you ever really match an OG?

The *#Hashtag* series as a whole grew into this whole world that has been beloved by so many readers. And to think it all started with a girl with bad fashion, clumsy feet, and a love for animals and the blue-eyed, blond-haired charmer who was dared to "have sex with the #nerd."

I think part of the appeal of *#Nerd* is that Rimmel is so relatable. She is awkward, loves to read, prefers books and animals to people, and is just herself. It's a classic tale of opposites attract with some drama thrown in. Plus, she lives in sweats. Hello, comfy clothes!

Thank you for the support over the last decade. This series has far surpassed what I ever anticipated. I hope you have enjoyed this novella updating you on your favorite family and also the small cameos of other beloved characters! The *#Hashtag* fam is still going strong and will be for many, many years to come.

No one does it quite like Romeo, am I right? *Hells yeah!*

It's truly an honor to be here after all this time, and I definitely wouldn't have made it this far without you.

Here's to the next decade…
Cambria

ABOUT CAMBRIA HEBERT

Cambria Hebert is a bestselling novelist of more than seventy titles. She went to college for a bachelor's degree, couldn't pick a major, and ended up with a degree in cosmetology. So rest assured her characters will always have good hair.

Besides writing, Cambria loves a pumpkin spice latte, staying up late, sleeping in, and watching movies until her eyes won't stay open. She considers math human torture and has an irrational fear of chickens (yes, chickens). You can often find her running on the treadmill (she'd rather be eating a donut), painting her toenails, or walking her chihuahuas (the real bosses of the house).

Cambria has written in many genres, including new adult, sports romance, male/male romance, sci-fi, thriller, suspense, contemporary romance, and young adult. Many of her titles have been translated into foreign languages and have been the recipient of multiple awards.

Awards Cambria has received include:

Author of the Year 2016 (UtopiaCon2016)
The Hashtag Series: Best Contemporary Series of 2015
(UtopiaCon 2015)
#Nerd: Best Contemporary Book Cover of 2015 (UtopiaCon
2015)
Romeo from the Hashtag Series: Best Contemporary Lead
(UtopiaCon 2015)
#Nerd: Top 50 Summer Reads (Buzzfeed.com 2015)
The Hashtag Series: Best Contemporary Series of 2016
(UtopiaCon 2016)
#NERD Book Trailer: Best Book Trailer of 2016 (UtopiaCon
2016)
#Nerd Book Trailer: Top 50 Most Cinematic Book Trailers
of All Time (film-14.com)
#Nerd: Book Most Wanted to be Adapted to Screen (2018)
Amnesia: Mystery Book of the Year (2018)
Red: Best LGBTQIA+ Book of the Year (2022)

Cambria Hebert owns and operates Cambria Hebert
Books, LLC.

You can find out more about Cambria and her titles by
visiting her website:
http://www.cambriahebert.com
Stay up to date on all of Cambria's new releases and more by
signing up for her newsletter: https://view.flodesk.com/
pages/62bf54af9b2a0dd45de3fa82